# JONATHAN
# DOWN
# UNDER

# Patricia Beatty

# JONATHAN DOWN UNDER

William Morrow and Company
New York 1982

Printed in the United States of America.

1  2  3  4  5  6  7  8  9  10

Library of Congress Cataloging in Publication Data

Beatty, Patricia
  Jonathan down under.

  Summary: Thirteen-year-old Jonathan accompanies his luckless miner father to the gold fields of Australia, where he learns to be his own man amidst the rough-and-ready society of nineteenth-century Victoria.
  [1. Australia—Fiction.  2. Gold mines and mining—Fiction]
I. Title.
PZ7.B380544Jo  1982  [Fic]  82-8245
ISBN 0-688-01467-4

To
the Australian couple
who showed me Ballarat,
Ada ("Madam") Barnes
and
Ralph Barnes
(that "Wild Colonial Boy,"
actually born in Castlemaine)

# Contents

# 1

## An Unexpected Port

"China!" whispered the boy under his breath. His delight in the very name transfigured his face. By the Great Horn Spoon, at this very moment he was on his way to China, bound for the exotic city of Shanghai on the far side of the world. His father said it was a place where remarkable yellow-skinned people made things of wondrous beauty. He could not believe his good fortune. China! This is where his and father's fortunes lay for the next few months—in the fabulous trading ports of China.

Suddenly he heard his name called. "Jonathan! Hey, son." Small, towheaded Jonathan Cole left the clipper ship's rail, where he'd stood for the last half hour happily watching the green water stream past the hull of the *Constance Moyle*.

Where was Charlie, his father? Ah, there he was, aft, with
the sea wind blowing his thinning fair hair. He was with a
knot of fellow passengers. He was laughing, gesturing, talking with his long-fingered hands. The men with him were
grinning, watching him. People often smiled when little
Charlie Cole got talking. It was only the first day of the long
passage and already he'd attracted the attention of other
voyagers. And how he loved an audience!

For a few minutes, thirteen-year-old Jonathan watched
him, standing unnoticed on the rising and falling deck. He
thought of his father's luck, which had changed once again
from bad to good not six days past. As he'd often heard his
father say, "There's no telling about Dame Fortune,
Johnny. First she curses a man, then she smiles on him."

As he saw his father's happiness, Jonathan smiled too. The
smile made his usually sober face come alive. It pointed up
his strong resemblance to his father, though the older Cole,
who did not get into fist fights, was not missing his right
front tooth as Jonathan was.

The memory of receiving the letter from Massachusetts
six days ago was the cause of this moment's happy, gap-
tooth grin. That letter had been three months coming from
Boston to their mining claim near the town of French Camp
in California. It had carried both the news that Jonathan's
bachelor great-uncle, a mill owner, had died the year before,
and that his estate finally had been settled. He had left Jonathan's father a legacy of three hundred dollars, and the Cole
family lawyer had enclosed a bank draft for the amount. At
once Charlie Cole had said the draft was "a gift from Dame
Fortune" and "very welcome too." Jonathan had agreed. It

12

had come in the nick of time, because the Coles had reached the very bottom of their purse.

"Jonathan. Come here," rose the man's voice again, breaking in on his son's thoughts.

Holding onto the rail, Jonathan came up to his father and the men with him. Charlie Cole's bright blue eyes were shining as he flung one arm over his son's shoulder and swung him about to face the other men. "This is my boy, Johnny. He's . . ." Cole would have gone on, but just at the moment a freshening wind struck the great square white sails of the *Constance Moyle,* making them explode with a loud boom that drowned out his voice. He waited, then said, "As I started to say, this is my son, who left the family farm near Pittsfield, Massachusetts, with me in 1849 for California when we got word of the gold strike. He mined with me in French Camp for two years, didn't you, Johnny?"

"Sure, Pa."

"You bet Johnny did. He panned and dug and he cooked for both of us."

A heavyset, brown-bearded man said, "I left my claim because I never saw one speck of gold in two years' time. What made you leave yours?"

"Ah!" Charlie Cole held up a forefinger. Jonathan knew this sign of old. It meant his father was warming to a tale. Whenever he did this, the boy kept quiet to listen too; sometimes what his father said could be mighty interesting. "Gentlemen, we were weary of digging. We had found enough gold to leave—to sell our claim and begin a new venture. This one will be of more benefit to my boy than mining. It will take us to San Francisco to live so that he can

13

be educated as befits his intelligence. He is a very smart boy. He has not gone to school for two years because we had lived a goodly distance from any town. With the gold we'd found, I bought two round-trip tickets to China for my boy and myself."

The bearded passenger asked, "Why take him to China if you're so interested in getting schooling for him? Couldn't you have left him in Frisco with his mother?"

"No, sir. My poor Johnny's motherless. My wife took a fever and died when he was just a baby. I raised him." Jonathan felt his father's arm tighten around his shoulder. "Johnny and me, that's all there is of the Coles out here in California. And we stick together. So he goes with me to China, where I'll buy the sort of things the ladies in Frisco like—ivories, porcelains, and silks. I plan to set up an import shop on Market Street as soon as we get back."

Another passenger, a red-faced man who wore a black plug hat, took a cigar out of his mouth and said, "Yep, there'd be a good bit of money to be made in sellin' cloth the way the ladies dress themselves. My wife's skirts have got so wide lately that she goes sideways through the back door. To make a gown for her takes plenty of cloth."

"Exactly. Exactly, sir!" exclaimed Charlie Cole.

The brown-bearded man poked Jonathan in the chest and asked, "So, you did dang well in the mines, huh?"

"Yes, sir," said the boy, agreeing with the lie his father had just told. Clearly his father didn't want these men to know how poorly they had done and that they would soon have had to ask someone for a grubstake to keep them digging at all. These well-dressed gentlemen were men his father sought to impress. He wanted them to believe he had done very well mining and that they would be well served if their wives shopped at his store on Market Street.

The red-faced passenger said to Jonathan, "I happen to hail from Massachusetts myself. I take it you didn't like farming there?"

"No, sir, I didn't," cried the boy, who was forced to yell into the rising wind. The Cole farm had been a cheerless place of rocks and hard winters, and the school he'd trudged five miles to was a place of torment. As the smallest boy in his class, he'd been the victim of bigger schoolmates. It had been a relief not to have to go to school in California. The Coles' mining claim had been too far from the actual town for the truant officer to come seeking him.

A third passenger shouted now, "The wind's getting too strong for talking out here on deck. I'm goin' into the salon," and he pointed to the bow of the ship.

Charlie Cole called out, "Sure, let's go inside. I'd like to tell you gentlemen what I have in mind to do once I've made my profits in the China trade. I'm a man of plans myself."

Jonathan tugged at his father's coat sleeve. "Pa, let me stay on deck. I like it out here."

Cole laughed. "Of course, son. Stay out here in the fresh air; but if you start to feel chilly, go below to our cabin till you hear the call for dinner." He now let go of Jonathan's shoulder and with the other passengers filed forward, each man holding onto the rail, bending against the wind.

Once they'd gone, Jonathan turned to look out over the white-capped sea again. Because it was September, sunset would come soon and after this, his first night aboard the clipper ship. They'd sailed through the Golden Gate and had already passed the Farallon Islands. A glance astern showed only ocean; the California coast was gone, not to be seen again for months.

Suddenly Jonathan shivered. The wind was getting colder and colder. A thin spray thrown up from the sea caught him in the face and on the hands, chilling them. Listening to the rattling of the clipper's rigging and the creaking of her masts, he made his way across the deck to the open hatchway that led below. He went down the companionway steps and along the lower deck until he reached the cabin door. Opening it, he stepped high over the coaming so as not to stumble, went inside, and closed the door after him.

Though he could have his choice of either empty berth, he climbed into the top one. Sleeping so high in the air was an adventure in itself. He lay there, his arms folded over his chest, feeling the rolling and pitching of the ship. A warm glow of happiness enveloped him in the tiny, wood-paneled cabin. Here he was aboard a Baltimore-built new Yankee clipper, the finest, most beautiful, swiftest ship in the world, and on his way to China, a place of fables. He was no longer poor. Jonathan Cole chuckled aloud. By the Great Horn Spoon, he would have adventures aplenty in China!

One glorious day followed another. He suffered little from seasickness. The *Constance Moyle* was a wondrous world. One of the cabin boys, Matthew, who had already made a China voyage, took him under his wing. Matthew listened with interest to Jonathan's account of how he'd lost a fight in San Francisco just before he boarded the clipper, and sympathized with him on the loss of a front tooth. While Charlie Cole talked in the salon or played whist with the adult passengers, Jonathan roamed the clipper with the snub-nosed cabin boy. Matthew wanted to be an able seaman someday, so had learned much about ships. He told Jonathan what hours the ship's bells represented, what such calls as "Square the foreyard" and "Man the weather braces" meant. Jonathan and Matthew watched sunsets and the even more beautiful ocean sunrises. Once Matthew even took him up into the rigging until the second mate angrily ordered both boys down. At night the two of them sat side by side on a hatch cover listening to the ship's noises. Matthew pointed out the stars navigators used to plot a course at sea. Jonathan learned how to find the North Star by sighting along the Big Dipper and to identify Sirius, brightest of all stars, Rigel in the constellation Orion, and others. Matthew even taught him the words of sea chanteys and told him that if they wanted to, the passengers would be permitted to fish for sharks with pork-baited lines when they came into waters near the Sandwich Islands. To think of catching a shark on a hook!

It seemed to Jonathan that his father was pleased with the voyage too. One night while they lay in their berths some ten days out of San Francisco, he heard his father ask from below, "You like this ship, eh, Johnny?"

"Oh, yes, Pa."

"So do I. The captain says if we're lucky in the winds we may make a new record for the fastest voyage ever to China, less than six weeks' time. The winds have been with the ship for days now. The faster we get to China, the faster we get back to Frisco, huh, and start out in business?"

Jonathan's words were less joyful now. "I guess so." He wanted the voyage to last forever, but of course that wasn't possible, because nothing went on forever.

Cole said, "You know, there's a man aboard who's already in the importing business. He tells me the profits could be a mite slower than I think. It won't be like prospecting, where any day can be the luckiest and richest of a man's entire life. He said that it takes a heap of time to build up a lot of customers in a store."

"Maybe so."

"Well, son, it's something to think about, isn't it?"

"I reckon it is." Jonathan changed the subject to ask, "Pa, if we do fish for sharks, will you help me hold my line?"

"Of course I will. Don't we do everything together?"

From having seen two tiny white specks on the far-distant horizon the next day, Jonathan realized that there were other ships sailing the same sea lanes as the *Constance Moyle*. Matthew Briggs, who had borrowed a spyglass from the second mate, reported that the tiny dots were really a schooner and a bark.

No ship ever came near enough for anyone to make out a name, however, until the afternoon of the day the clipper was due to make port at nightfall in the Sandwich Islands. At the rail as usual, Jonathan saw a ship coming toward them, traveling south to cross the clipper's bow. The westerly winds that prevailed here drove the stranger at a swift passing slant, and her speed made the boy catch his breath and wonder if she would collide with the *Constance Moyle*.

This was no sleek clipper but a smaller, clumsier vessel that rose higher in the water than the *Constance Moyle*. The ship was battered and in need of paint.

He heard the second mate tell an inquiring passenger who stood nearby, "She's a whaler by the look of her, and she's flying the American flag. I say she'd hail from Nantucket or New Bedford." Jonathan saw him lift the spyglass to his eye, then heard him say, "She's the *Wendover* out of Nantucket."

As he watched the other ship, Jonathan suddenly saw a small flag hoisted to the tip of one of her mastheads. At the sight of it the second mate walked swiftly to the stern, where the clipper ship's captain maintained his majestic aloneness. Watching the *Wendover*, Jonathan saw that the moment after the small flag had been raised, sailors started up into her rigging to shorten sail, to bring the whaler to a standstill on the open sea. Why?

By now Matthew had come to stand with Jonathan. "What's going on?" he asked the cabin boy.

"I don't know for sure, but I think we'll stop too." Matthew sounded excited. "Maybe it's to be a gam, a sort of visiting ship-to-ship that whaling captains do with one another at sea. But maybe not. It could be they've got a sick man aboard and want us to take him with us to the Sandwich Islands to be cared for by the medical missionaries there."

The *Constance Moyle* too halted on the ocean. The seamen of the clipper went aloft and shortened her load of sail, then threw out her sea anchors. In a short time the two ships lay together, drifting slightly on a gently heaving sea of ever-deepening blue. Jonathan saw one of the whaler's boats lowered away and rowed toward the clipper.

Only one person climbed the clipper's ladder, a tall man in a black frock coat and high hat. When only one came visiting, this was clearly no whaler captain's gam. As the stranger stepped onto the deck, Jonathan became aware that his father now stood behind him, listening.

The newcomer from the *Wendover* said in a loud voice, "Captain Appleby's my name, owner and master of the brig *Wendover*. I saw by your flag that this is a Yankee ship. Because I'm a Yankee too, I think it's my duty to bring you the news I got yesterday from an English schooner bound from Singapore to Chile. That news made me change my course, let me tell you."

"News?" asked Charlie Cole sharply. "My God, is America at war, sir?"

Jonathan caught his breath. War? Yes, that would be the sort of news any ship captain would stop midocean to tell another from his country.

"No, not war. Gold! It's news of gold, the biggest strike the world's ever seen."

"Where's the gold?" cried Charlie Cole over all the other excited voices, for by now a number of other passengers were also on the deck.

"Down under. In Australia. At a place called Ballarat. As I said, I've changed my ship's course for Australia. My crew and I are quitting whaling. I hope to sell the *Wendover* there. There's no time now for whales when the nuggets in Ballarat run to nine pounds. I saw one with my own eyes yesterday. A passenger bound for Chile had bought it from the Australian who found it."

Jonathan felt his father's hands grip him by the shoulders. He heard him ask, his words exploding from his mouth,

"Will you take my son and me with you to Australia? I'll pay you good money for the passage."

"But, Pa, we're going to China!" cried Jonathan, looking from his father's flushed face to the captain's.

Neither man paid any heed to him. After a moment's reflection, the captain said, "Aye, there'd be some room for you in the foc'sle if you've got forty dollars to give me. Have your gear ready to shove off in the longboat with me once I've given my news to the captain of this vessel."

"We'll be ready to go with you, sir."

Looking around the group of passengers, Captain Appleby said, "I can make room for another one of you men if you pay me now. I'll need some cash if I can't sell my ship straight away in Australia."

An excited passenger said loudly, "I dug for gold in California too. I'd go with you in a minute if I didn't have all my money tied up in the China trade and people waiting for me in Shanghai!"

Another passenger said, "Even if I never prospected a day in my life, I'd go with you if I could; but you'll never make me believe in nuggets that large."

The captain said, "I saw that gold. I lifted it. I'm a man of my word. It was nine pounds of pure gold."

Just before he went down the hatchway to the cabin he shared with his father, Jonathan heard the rumbling of the other passengers talking to each other. He had no time to talk below with his father about the sudden change in plans. The man forestalled that by saying, "Hurry up, son, pack your duds. Don't waste time talking. This is my chance of a lifetime, and I'm going to take it."

In a short time the Coles were waiting at the ladder of the

*Constance Moyle* with their small collection of baggage. Charlie Cole's passenger acquaintances clustered around to shake his hand, wish him luck, and say farewell. Several, Jonathan thought, looked enviously at his father as if they too wanted to go. Matthew pressed Jonathan's hand and wished him well, and Jonathan pretended that he was delighted to go.

Before long Captain Appleby returned and was climbing down the ship's ladder ahead of the Coles and into the boat. As the *Wendover*'s sailors bent to their oars, Jonathan twisted around on the seat to bid farewell with his eyes to the lovely clipper ship, trying to fix her grace in his mind forever.

Charlie Cole told him, "Don't look back, son. Forget China. Lord in heaven, how my luck has changed! A new gold strike—and the richest the world has ever known! Think of all the prospecting experience I got in the California goldfields! It isn't as if I know much about shopkeeping and the importing business. You know, I might have gone bust at that in Frisco and lost all of our money."

Ashamed of his misting eyes, Jonathan mumbled, "No, Pa, I won't look back."

Once more dreams of finding gold were running through his father's head. The China venture was over. Jonathan mourned its loss. After two years he'd come to dislike prospecting as backbreaking toil with no returns for all its trouble. To his way of thinking mining had been no better than farming in Massachusetts; and at least in Pittsfield there had been his father's sisters, who befriended and at times mothered him. In California there had been only his father, his plans, and his dreams. And now they were bound for yet another gold strike—this time in a strange land, where they would know no one but the men from the *Wendover*, who also were bound for down under. Down under what?

He stole a glance at his father and saw how his fists were knotted on his knees. He saw the odd light in his eyes and recognized the very self-willed look his face had worn at times in California when he'd wrongly sensed he was on the brink of a strike that would make him instantly rich. It was the look of obsession. He had seen many men with such an expression in the California mining country.

The Coles found the slower-sailing *Wendover* very different from the clipper ship. On the whaler they enjoyed no comfortable passenger's cabin; they had to sleep together in a berth in the cramped foc'sle, the crew's quarters. They also had to buy mugs, tin plates, cutlery, and blankets from the ship's slop chest at high prices. Where they had dined on fowl and pigs kept in pens on the deck of the clipper, here they ate the same dull fare day after day—salted beef, potatoes, ship's biscuit, beans, and coffee.

For the first three days of the voyage, the pitching of the whaler and the greasy food forced Jonathan again and again to the rail to vomit with seasickness. After that his stomach accepted the change of ships, but not his heart. He hungered for the *Constance Moyle,* by now many sea miles north by west of the *Wendover* on her way to China.

Worse though than the food and stagnant air of the foc'sle was the sullenness of the *Wendover*'s crew. The captain was not to be approached, and there was no Matthew Briggs here to befriend Jonathan. At first he did not understand the reason for the crew's hostility; but one day when he took

23

two flying fish that had landed on the deck to the ship's cook, he was told the reason. The cook, an old man, snarled at the sight of the fish and said, "So, ya got weary of salt beef already, huh, and ya want me to fry these here fish for ya special? Well, I ain't about to do that. Throw 'em over the side. It's the captain's idea that you and your pa are aboard this ship, not mine or the crew's. Captain Appleby took your passage money. He didn't give any of it to us or ask us first about takin' ya aboard. But captains don't treat crews like anythin' other than dirt.

"We found out that you and yer pa dug for gold before you come aboard. So you got to know how to go about it. None of us sailors do. You two stand a lot better chance of gettin' rich than we do. You can't expect us to welcome anybody aboard who's goin' to have a head start on us in pickin' up big nuggets. A couple of crew members asked yer pa to let us in on how you do that kind of work, and he said he wasn't goin' to tell us. Did you know that, boy?"

"No, sir." Still holding the fish, Jonathan stepped backward. He hadn't known that any of the crew had tried to question his father about prospecting.

Jonathan left the cookshack, astonished at the man's hostility, dropped the still-wriggling flying fish over the rail, and went to find his father. He was sitting at the tiny table in the foc'sle, playing a solitary card game. Jonathan said, "Pa, the cook told me just now that the crew don't like you and me because we've prospected before. Maybe if you told the sailors what you know about hunting for gold, they'd be more friendly."

Charlie Cole looked up from his cards, shook his head, and said, "No, Johnny, two of them have already asked me.

I won't tell them anything. Why should I give them the benefit of two years' learning. Don't you tell them either if they ask you."

"All right." Johnny sighed and left to go to the rail and watch the sea, hoping to sight the porpoises he'd seen the day before. Their frolicking around the *Wendover* had lifted his spirits.

After three weeks' sailing, the *Wendover* reached the equator. From seamen's talk he overheard, Jonathan Cole learned what "down under" meant—down under the equator. Though he thought he'd known summer heat in Massachusetts, he now realized he had never experienced true hot weather. Three days becalmed on a windless sea taught him the miseries of tropical heat. The ship's drinking water stank, but he drank it eagerly when it was given to him. Everyone had to sleep on deck to breathe at all. No one talked of anything but the absent wind and how best to summon it. At last the surly old cook, whom Jonathan now avoided, burned his galley broom, saying that act had always fetched a breeze for him before.

The weather changed on the third day in the doldrums. That night the setting sun glowed like a red-hot iron stove lid below the black of a bank of low-lying clouds. Just after dark an equatorial squall hit the *Wendover* with a hissing rain. While thunder crashed overhead and flame-colored sheets of lightning circled the whaler as if mocking her, great white pearls of hail danced along the deck, forcing Jonathan and the others to take any shelter they could find from its stinging fury.

The next morning, though, brought blue skies, rolling

seas, and fresh winds. That day too Jonathan spied plumes of white spray off the port bow. He was told that the spray was whales spouting; but Captain Appleby did not lower whaleboats nor have the long, wickedly barbed harpoons taken down from where they hung.

The moon had been waxing when the Coles first boarded the *Wendover*. The whaler had been made beautiful by its silver light, and to Jonathan's eyes her rigging had seemed etched at night with hoarfrost, her sails snowlike, and the sea surrounding her a jet-black bowl with shimmering stripes. By the time the whaler had passed through the doldrums and the squall, however, the moon had disappeared from the sky and Jonathan saw a strange heaven above. Where the Big Dipper had dominated the sky he was familiar with, there was a new constellation, the Southern Cross. It was a line of brilliant white stars crossed near one end by another line at a slant. For some reason its very strangeness dismayed him. Until now Jonathan had never thought of a night sky as an old friend.

As they continued sailing south, it grew somewhat cooler, and the sailors who had sweated in cotton shirts and duck trousers donned jackets for warmth. The *Wendover* raced under full sail beneath a sky of such an eye-aching blue that it dazzled Jonathan and made his father say that he had never seen such a color. Nearing the east coast of Australia, the whaler battled rough seas and head winds, while the wind screeched in her rigging like a woman crying for a lost child.

One evening when the head winds had died down a bit, Jonathan, standing at his usual post at the rail, saw seabirds flying out of the south. Some perched atop the swaying mastheads of the *Wendover*. Members of the crew saw them too and clapped each other on the back. One man shouted out, "Land's near now!"

The next morning, after nearly three months of travel aboard two ships, Jonathan saw land off the starboard bow. It was only a blue-purple stain on the horizon then, but hour by hour it grew more distinct. By sunset of that day Jonathan could smell it, and what a strange scent Australia was, so pungent it made his nose wrinkle.

He called his father from his game of solitaire in the foc'sle to smell it too. Charlie Cole filled his nose with the odor, laughed, and cried, "Yes, it's land all right! Land can be smelled. They say the scent of flowers from a tropical island carries for miles out to sea. I heard the second mate say not five minutes ago that we're in the Bass Strait between the mainland of Australia and the big island of Van Diemen's Land to the south. That's the scent of gold you smell.

"You know, son, I just thought of something. It could be lucky for you here. Americans aren't only called Yankees by people in other lands but sometimes Brother Jonathans. You're already a Jonathan, so here you might be Brother Jonathan Down Under or just plain Johnny Down Under."

"That could be, Pa."

As he stared at the line of land on the horizon, Jonathan wondered about the Australians and the reception he and his father might get from them. He knew his American history from school. England ruled Australia, and America and England had fought two wars. Grandfather Cole had fought in that last war of 1812 and had carried a musket ball from it embedded in his shoulder. Perhaps the Australians wouldn't like foreigners digging in their land. Some American miners he'd known in California had resented the Chileans, Mexicans, and Europeans who had filed claims and dug for American gold.

Jonathan said, "Pa, the Australians might not want us."

Charlie Cole laughed. "The whole world flocks to every gold strike. If they don't know it yet, the Australians will soon find that out. I'll bet there'll be other Americans in Ballarat ahead of us. We won't be the only Brother Jonathans."

The boy said nothing. Instead he thought of the song the *Wendover*'s sailors had sung that very morning. It had been a rousing chantey, but the words had disturbed him. It was as though they had been aimed at him, as over and over they sang: "Leave her, Johnny, leave her."

# 2

## The Golden Window

In the morning Jonathan spied the little pilot ship sailing toward the *Wendover* in response to her flag signaling that a pilot was needed. He stayed at the rail to see the pilot come up the Jacob's ladder and guide the whaler through the dangerous passage between the narrow rocky heads at Port Phillip into Hobson's Bay. A southerly wind took the *Wendover* scudding past the narrows of the heads and swiftly over rough water into the bay.

At dawn of the next day Jonathan was again on deck, straining his eyes for a closer view of this new continent, expecting to see the city of Melbourne rise up on hills before him like San Francisco. He saw only a dark irregular shoreline that resolved itself into houseless hills and deep green forest, and then into a number of settlements scattered along the bay's wide shores. One settlement was sure to be Melbourne. Jonathan saw that not all ships had come through the heads safely. Wrecks littered the shores of the bay. Other vessels, their masts naked of sails, lay at anchor a distance from the beaches. Jonathan thought these ships strange looking. Their hulls were neither red nor black but yellow. Near them lay a black, sleek-hulled sloop with gunports for cannon below her top deck.

As Charlie Cole came out of the foc'sle, Jonathan asked, "What are the yellow ships?"

The agile little pilot who had stayed aboard the *Wendover* overnight answered Jonathan's question, startling him. "The hulks? They're convict ships. Convicts who build the stone wall at Gellibrand Point by day sleep aboard 'em at night—convicts sent out here to Australia from old England. I was one meself. Good day to ye."

Both Coles stared at the man, who laughed softly and added, "There'll be many ticket-of-leave men like myself at the mines and some far worse than me who never stole nothin' more in old England than thirteen boots."

"Thirteen pairs of boots?" asked Charlie Cole.

"Naw, thirteen boots."

"Why thirteen?"

Just before he swung out over the side, the Australian pilot grinned and said, "That's a thing for ye new chum Yankees to ponder while ye break yer backs at Ballarat along with ten thousand other diggers." And he was gone, down to his own boat waiting below, leaving the Coles looking at one another in astonishment.

Charlie Cole didn't talk about the thirteen boots. Instead he said, "This could turn out to be a queer country, Johnny. You know, it's early summer here now, though it's coming on to snowtime in Massachusetts. Summer means hot weather anywhere, though here the seasons happen to be upside down for us. One good thing about summer—we don't have to buy cold weather duds to take to the goldfields. We'll outfit for the mines in Melbourne. I heard the captain say Melbourne's supposed to be a real city, and it will be easy to get what we need there. It isn't as if we don't know just what a prospector needs anywhere, eh?"

"No, Pa. We know," said Jonathan, holding on to the rigging as he watched the pilot ship sail away, heading south to guide another ship through the heads. He was thinking of the pilot's words about convicts and ex-convicts in Australia. Surely they were criminals—murderers and thieves. What kind of land would this be if it held many who were criminals? A queer land indeed, and likely a dangerous one!

The *Wendover* docked at Queen's Wharf in Melbourne harbor early that afternoon, and the crew and officers of the ship swarmed down the gangplank. Moments later they were shouting "Which way to Ballarat?" to the only person in sight, a pipe-smoking old fellow sitting on a barrel on the wharf.

He took his pipe from his mouth, pointed to the west, and said, "Some two, three days' walk that way, about sixty, seventy miles." Then he put the pipe back into his mouth, clamping his teeth down on it.

Jonathan and his father didn't go after the sailors. Carry-

31

ing their carpetbags, the two of them walked up to the man, and Charlie Cole asked him where they could find a place to outfit for the goldfields.

The reply was, "Over the Yarra Yarra River. Go to Collins Street."

After thanking the old man, Jonathan saw his father look around him at the ships in the harbor. Some were rigged with sails but empty of men, lying at anchor like the deserted *Wendover.* He turned to Jonathan to say, "San Francisco was just like this in 1849. Everybody who's come to port here has jumped ship and gone to the mines."

"So they have," agreed the man on the barrel. "I'd go to Ballarat meself if I wasn't so lame. Diggers, that's what the men of Melbourne have become. 'Tis mostly a city of women and children now, but there's still some men here to keep order and to tend to business and see that the gold nuggets in the jeweler's windows don't get stole."

"*Nuggets?*" asked Charlie Cole.

"Aye, mate, nuggets what's been found in the goldfields. Go see for yerself; there's one on Collins Street."

"Thank you, sir. Thank you. Come on, Jonathan."

As they walked, the solid ground rose and fell under Jonathan's feet as if he were still aboard a ship. His father seemed too to stagger as if he were dizzy, but he said it would soon pass.

Beyond the wharf and the shelter of the warehouses, dusty winds struck the two Americans. They whirled hotly about them, blinding them, battering their faces, making Jonathan gasp for breath and lower his head to save his eyes. A rowboat they hailed took them over the Yarra Yarra

River, scattering a bevy of coal-black swans with its splashing oars. Once on the northern bank they walked again in the summer winds. Soon they were in the more populated parts of the town and sheltered from the gusts by taller buildings. Now Jonathan was able to look about himself. Just in time he leaped back with his father against a building as a pack of dogs ran past him in hot pursuit of a sleek young sow.

Eventually, they found Collins Street. Though Melbourne wasn't yet the fine city that Boston and San Francisco both were, it too boasted brick buildings as well as the more humble one- and two-story wooden ones. Jonathan saw a theater, shops, offices, banks, hotels, and cafés.

He also saw a goodly number of people. For the most part they were women out shopping with baskets over their arms. Their hoop skirts were as broad as those worn by women in San Francisco, and they looked much like the ladies there; but the men he saw did not dress like the sober San Franciscan males. These men wore white linen coats and trousers and light-colored felt hats, where the San Franciscans wore dark clothing and plug or top hats. Some of these Australian men wore odd-looking headgear made from some plaited fiber, not straw. The men walked past the Coles, intent on their own affairs, showing no interest in the newcomers. Some ladies, though, smiled at Jonathan, who politely took off his hat and smiled in return.

Suddenly, Jonathan saw his father stop up ahead, drop his carpetbags in the dust, and stare into a shop window. Jonathan watched his mouth open and his eyes glaze over and heard him croak, "Look, son!"

The boy came up and looked into the same window. There on a piece of blue cloth lay a big, irregularly shaped chunk of pitted, pockmarked metal. Gold! It was gold! An enormous nugget, so large it was unbelievable. Under it was a white card with the written words, *Found at Ballarat, October 1851.*

Jonathan Cole felt himself starting to tremble. His knees were about to buckle under him, and he began to breathe faster. A wild sensation came over him in a rush, and his reflected face in the window glass looked exactly as his father's did at that moment. At last he'd felt the surging passion known as gold fever. The sheer size of the Australian nugget had done this to him, where the small California nuggets and gold dust he'd seen had not.

"Look at it!" whispered his father, half to himself, half to Jonathan. Then he struck the boy on the back and said, "Tear your eyes away from it and let's go buy what we'll need to find a beauty like this for ourselves."

Dazed, Jonathan took up the carpetbags he had also dropped and after one long look at the nugget shining splendidly in the window went after his father. Perhaps he was right that their luck was going to be better here in Australia, where men found gold in such a big way. One nugget as large as the one in the window could surely send them home to America rich men. Who knew how long it would take them to find a big nugget? Certainly it had not taken some men long, for gold hadn't been discovered in Ballarat until just six months ago and look what had already been found!

Jonathan quickened his pace to catch up to his father, who was striding briskly along, smiling and nodding at the Melbourne ladies they passed. The boy guessed at the cause of his happy behavior. Charlie Cole was thinking he would be early on the scene in Ballarat; and, because he was an experienced prospector, he would have an advantage over all the others who came ignorant and later. Jonathan agreed with him. That meeting at sea between the *Constance Moyle* and the whaler had been a truly lucky chance, a gift from Dame Fortune. They had been right to abandon the China venture for something at which they were both better fitted.

After the Coles had changed their dollars to pounds, shillings, and pence at a bank on Collins Street, they went to the shop the bank clerk had recommended to buy the shovels, picks, and buckets they would need at Ballarat. The items were expensive, but the shop clerk said they were cheaper here than they would be in the goldfields. She was a talkative, gray-haired woman. When she advised them to buy a tent, she said, "You'll be able to sell it for three times what ye paid for it if ye decide to leave the diggings." She added, "It would be best for ye if ye do not start for Ballarat till daybreak though, when others will be going there."

"Why not go now, ma'am?" asked Charlie Cole.

"Because it's not safe to travel alone or go by two's or three's. There be bushrangers on the road, highwaymen who shout at ye, 'Bail up,' then rob and shoot ye dead. The Black Forest's noted for 'em. 'Tis a place ye must pass through, 'tis the shortest way to Ballarat."

Jonathan saw his father's eyes widen as the older Cole said, "I surely would not have known what 'bail up' meant. Thank you, ma'am. Let me ask you this. How safe is Melbourne by night?"

*Jonathan Down Under*

" 'Tis safe enough. There's good order kept here. Now, sir, if ye go three doors down this same street, ye can buy the food supplies ye want. Tea costs a small fortune in Ballarat, I'm told, and so does flour."

"Thank you once more. Could you also tell me where to rent a wagon and horse to take us to the mines tomorrow?"

She laughed. "There's no call for a wagon when I can sell ye wheelbarrows that ye can use now and when ye get there. Ye'll have no need of a horse or cart in Ballarat."

A wheelbarrow? Jonathan's face fell at the prospect of pushing a barrow for days, but his father said, "What a capital idea! I'll need two barrows then. Now where can we get supper and spend the night?"

"At the Sailor's Rest in Canvas Town over the Yarra Yarra. 'Tis clean and safe and a good bit cheaper than the Lamb Inn unless ye plan to lodge in style. If ye go to Canvas Town, ye'll be certain to find other folk going out to Ballarat in the morning."

Jonathan asked, "Will there be convicts there, ma'am?"

She gave him a level look, then said, "The man who keeps the Sailor's Rest is, like meself and me husband, transported. We was all transported years ago from English gaols to New South Wales on our promises never to go back home to England. But convicts here in Australia we never was; we came here free. Not all here were transported, if that's what ye be thinking. Some came of their own free will. Some were born here. Those who are born in New South Wales we call cornstalks. We're all kinds of folk here in Australia. I hear ye be all kinds in America too."

"Indeed we are all kinds, ma'am," came from Charlie Cole, who gave Jonathan a reproving look. "My boy meant no harm in what he said. He's weary. Thank you for all your help. Come along, son."

Canvas Town was a tent city of people making ready for the goldfields. A night in the large tent called Sailor's Rest refreshed the Coles and gave them back their "land legs." They started out in the morning at sunrise, trudging their wheelbarrows. Twenty others, eighteen men and two women, left with them.

At the banks of the Yarra Yarra, Jonathan spied a group of dark-skinned people seated under a large, solitary gum tree as if they were waiting to cross. They were dressed exotically in a mixture of rags and bright-colored finery. Though one man wore a high silk hat, he had a stick inserted through the septum of his nose. All four individuals were barefooted and gazed with large, round black eyes at the party of gold seekers.

"Who are they?" Jonathan asked his father.

A man who'd been a tentmate of theirs the night before answered, "Blackfellows. Natives."

"Are they slaves?" asked the boy, still staring at the black people, who stared back at him.

The man, who came from Van Diemen's Land, said, "No, lad, they be free black men, not slaves as in America where ye hail from. All men Queen Victoria rules be free, save convicts. No man here owns a blackfellow."

"I am very glad to hear that, sir," said Charlie Cole, who like most Massachusetts citizens was against slavery. "I'm pleased to hear that your blackfellows are well treated by you!"

No one said anything, but several men waiting to be

ferried over the river with the Coles laughed. Charlie Cole, being agreeable, laughed with them, and so did Jonathan. As they passed through Melbourne, more gold seekers joined them. Some came with bedrolls slung over their shoulders and with mongrel dogs at their heels. Some drove balking and braying donkeys piled high with equipment and supplies. Others rode on horseback or in spring carts. At the outskirts of the city the carters, known as bullockies, joined the lines of travelers, walking beside their heavy, two-wheeled freight carts filled with supplies for Ballarat's storekeepers. As they walked they loudly cursed the oxen that pulled their carts, or cracked bullwhips over their heads to keep the animals moving. The Coles, in the center of the throng, were by no means the only people pushing laden wheelbarrows. The din made Jonathan wince. Shovels and buckets had been hung anywhere they could be, and how they clanked with every step!

In spite of the day's heat and searing gusts of wind, Charlie Cole was in a fine state of mind. Walking beside Jonathan, he would call out instructions. "Keep your barrow's wheel out of the ruts, Johnny. Don't let it tip over or we'll have to stop and fall behind the other folks."

Jonathan, who often found it hard to see through the powdery dust, nodded and shouted over the clamor as he struggled with his loaded barrow, "Pa, I'll try to keep out of the ruts." Despite his best efforts though, his barrow's one wheel would fall into rut after rut or become snagged on a tree root sprawling over the road. Then his father would come to help him.

At those times Charlie Cole would always say, "Just

think, Johnny, we're getting closer to those big nuggets with every step we take. Just think of what it'll be like to come back to California as rich as kings."

"It'll be fine."

"You bet it will." Then Cole would go back to his barrow, take it up, and move on, often turning his head to look at Jonathan and grin. Sometimes he'd make a face as if he too hated the fearful racket of the procession. Now and then he'd jerk his chin toward the hazy blue sky, calling Jonathan's attention to the shrieking blackbirds, magpies, and bold currawongs that swooped over the strung-out travelers.

Though no one in particular led the gold seekers and gave orders to halt at intervals, the procession sometimes stopped of its own accord to rest. The first time it did, Jonathan let his barrow down, wiped his forehead with his sleeve, and looked up from the deep dust of the road. The Australian countryside about him was pretty now, with grassy meadows on either side of him and in the distance low blue hills that invited an adventurous boy to climb them. Even though he would have liked to wander and explore a bit, he stayed beside his barrow, recalling what the lady in Melbourne had said about bushrangers. He stifled a groan as he moved his arms up and down to exercise them. His neck and back also ached. He wondered if he'd be able to straighten up at all by nightfall.

Later in the morning they halted again, this time in a shady place where trees bordered the road. Looking around, Charlie Cole commented, "Well, it's green here, but it surely isn't Massachusetts or California. Would you just look at those trees here on this side, the ones that look like huge ferns. And see those tall ones with the queer, smooth trunks across the way. Some of them are yellow, while the others are piebald black and gray." Jonathan watched his father cross the road and go up to a yellow-trunked tree, reach up, and pull down a leaf. He crumpled it, sniffed, and then came back holding it out to Jonathan. "Here, this is what we smelled out to sea."

Jonathan smelled the leaf of the eucalyptus, or gum tree, as the Australians called them, and nodded at the familiar pungent odor. Then he looked up at the tree nearest him. It was a fernlike tree and was indeed called a fern tree. Four galahs, large, rose-breasted birds, were perched on limbs high from the ground. The branches above them made a black lace pattern against a blue sky. What a colorful sight!

Hearing a sharp yelping, Jonathan looked behind him to see two yellow dogs on a low hilltop a distance away. Because he liked dogs he whistled to them to come, but at his whistle they turned and went trotting over the top of the hill and out of sight. They sure weren't friendly.

Suddenly he heard his father say, "Jonathan, I take to these fine trees. I never saw anything like them before. I bet they'd grow just dandy back in California. I'd like to take some of each back to San Francisco with us. They'd look nice in the yard of the house we'll build. You know, I bet you that we'll see a number of fine things before we get to Ballarat."

Jonathan wasn't interested in trees. His hands ached from the blisters the wheelbarrow handles had given him. So, Pa had fancied the trees? That was understandable; but hadn't he also seen things that morning that had made him look away instantly—the rotting, drying-out carcasses of dead horses and bullocks, pitiful reminders of earlier journeys to Ballarat? There had been graves too, three of them beside the road with rough crosses of wood over them.

The boy wanted to talk about these things to try and relieve his fears. So Jonathan asked, "Pa, didn't you see the dead animals and the graves along the road?"

"I saw them, but a man with ambitions can't let those things stop him, can he? Perhaps the animals and the men weren't well enough to tackle such a journey. If so, they should not have been on this road. That's only common sense, isn't it?"

"I reckon so." And Jonathan sighed.

At nightfall the weary travelers camped beside the road in a broad meadow. Jonathan sat at their small fire with his father and a married couple from New South Wales. Charlie Cole had made their acquaintance when he bought cold roast mutton from them for supper and, finding them friendly, asked them to share his campfire. To the Coles' surprise the middle-aged man and his plump little wife weren't bound for the mines. They were going to a sheep farm beyond Ballarat, where they had been hired as a shepherd and a cook.

Mr. and Mrs. Manwaren were interesting people, filled with information about their land. In spite of being weary from travel, they were willing to answer Jonathan's questions. He was curious about some creatures he had seen during the afternoon rest period. They looked like gray lumps, sitting high up in tall trees. Certainly they weren't birds, for when his father struck the tree trunks they had not flapped away.

Mrs. Manwaren told the Coles that they were koalas; she added, "They live up in the tall gum trees with never a drop of water but what they get from the leaves."

Her red-faced husband winked at Jonathan and said, "Leave a koala be and he'll leave you be. There's other things ye'd best be wary of too."

"What are they?" asked Jonathan quickly.

"The dingo dogs for one. Didn't ye see them atop the hill when we stopped this morning? There was a pair of them a'watching us."

Jonathan reflected, then said, "I saw yellow dogs that had tails curling up over their backs. I thought they were farm dogs."

"Not a bit of it, lad. They were dingoes, sheep-killin' wild dogs."

Now Charlie Cole entered the conversation with, "There are a number of poisonous snakes in our land. Do you have any here?"

Mrs. Manwaren's eyes rolled in her head. "Serpents, sir? Aye, beware of any snake ye see. Don't mind the lizards, though, no matter how big they are. Count the legs; and if there's four of 'em, ye'll be safe."

"Thank you, ma'am; Jonathan and I will be sure to be careful." Then Cole changed the subject before Jonathan could ask any more questions. "Tell us, please, have you seen any huge nuggets from Ballarat?"

"Aye, man, we have indeed," said Mr. Manwaren. "We saw three great ones in Sydney Town; but though I was tempted by them, I am no miner. I will work with the thing

I know best of all, sheep. Before gold was found at Ballarat, it was sheep farming that was the wealth of Australia."

Charlie Cole protested, "But it takes so long to raise a sheep and for a farmer to make a profit. It also takes land, acres of grazing land."

The woman asked, "Would ye know about farming?"

"Oh, yes, I had a farm in Massachusetts, which is on the east coast of the United States. I raised some sheep myself, so I know a bit about sheep farming."

"But ye'd rather go for gold?" asked the man.

"Indeed, sir. I tried farming for twenty years and it was not to my liking, though my father had done it before me and his father before him. I went out to California in the gold rush of 1849. What man with any adventure in his soul would not?" Spreading his hands, Charlie Cole grinned in the firelight. "So when I heard of the gold strike in Ballarat, I left a ship bound for China midocean to come to Australia. After I've made my fortune digging here, we'll return not to Massachusetts but to California."

Manwaren asked, "What will ye do there?"

"I shall go into business for myself, first open a shop in San Francisco, then in Sacramento, and after that in Monterey. I will sell only the best of goods, so no man can ever say that Charlie Cole cheated him when it came to quality."

Jonathan, who had heard all this before, closed his mind to the conversation and ate the cold mutton and the half-cooked potato. While the three adults continued talking, he got a blanket from his barrow, rolled up in it, and fell asleep beside the dying fire.

The next day the Coles and the Manwarens traveled together. Jonathan had to clench his teeth against the pain in his muscles as he pushed his wheelbarrow beside Mrs. Manwaren, who led one of the couple's two donkeys. Her husband and Charlie Cole walked in front of them.

It was Mrs. Manwaren who had roused Jonathan at daybreak to point out the group of red animals browsing a distance away on the left side of the road. "What are they?" he'd asked, pushing the blanket off him. Their faces looked a little like deer as they lifted their heads at a sound from the wakening camp. Then, in astonishment, Jonathan watched them rise up on their hind legs like humans with their small front legs dangling handlike. They stood without moving for a second; then in a body they whirled and leaped away, moving on powerful rear legs in great bounds into a grove of gum trees.

"What are they?" Jonathan had asked.

"Kangaroos, lad. Kangaroo tails make good soup. Ye see the creatures in the mornin' and at dusk. In the daytime they sleep."

Jonathan had heard his father say from beside him, "Remarkable beasts, aren't they?" He'd laughed. "My body would like to sleep all day too, but my brain tells me to cover the miles to Ballarat. Come on, let's get some breakfast into us and be on our way."

This day's journey brought the travelers to the notorious Black Forest the Melbourne shopkeeper had warned them of. The wide forest, which appeared as a dark wall from afar, well deserved its name. It was an eerie place— chill, somber, and damp. It was silent except for the call of some unseen bird that sang with a bell-like purity that made Jonathan shiver as he listened to it. He sensed that the shopkeeper had been correct in saying that the Black Forest was inhabited. He felt eyes on him from behind the tall trees, and the back of his neck prickled when he thought he heard a man's whistling and deep, mocking laughter. Mrs. Manwaren too must have known the forest was dangerous, because Jonathan saw how she often moved her head, glancing nervously from one close-growing, dark green tree to another. No one spoke. Nor did any of the dogs bark; they slunk along, their tails low, watching the bushes beneath the trees and sometimes running their tongues over their muzzles.

There was only one mishap in the awesome forest. A bullock cart became mired in a deep hole. Several of the men came over to it at once and helped the driver free it as swiftly as possible to keep the procession moving. While they pushed and strained, Jonathan stood silent beside his wheelbarrow next to Mrs. Manwaren. Both of them waited in an anxious silence for the cart to start on its way once more. When it did, the woman looked at Jonathan and gave him a crooked little smile of relief.

Beyond the Black Forest there were more rolling meadowlands and scattered gum trees and wattles in cheerful, bright yellow bloom. At the sight of them, everyone's spirits seemed to lift.

That night the Coles camped again with the Manwarens, but all four were too weary to talk at any length. However, after they'd eaten more cold mutton and potatoes cooked in the fire, Charlie Cole did tell Jonathan privately, "Remember what I said to you. Keep your mind on nuggets. My hands are just as blistered as yours are, but I reckon we've come some fifty miles. Tomorrow we'll be in Ballarat. Who knows what will happen on tomorrow's march."

Jonathan's first adventure came early in the morning. An hour away from the campsite of the night before, a trumpet blast alerted him to something unusual. Then came a loud shouting and the words, "Make way! Make way!" After that came a thunder and a clattering.

The bullockies all reined in their teams to the far side of the road and brought them to a halt. Everyone else too scurried to the edge of the roadway, lining it and holding fast to the halters of donkeys and horses. Standing beside their wheelbarrows, the Coles witnessed a very strange sight heading toward them. The first things they saw were two blue-coated soldiers, swords drawn and flashing, galloping past them. Then amid a furious clattering came a high-sided, two-wheeled cart pulled by four horses and driven by a man wielding a whip. Four more troopers with swords rode beside it, matching their speed to its. Behind came two more soldiers, similarly armed. And then the procession was gone, leaving clouds of dust behind it so high that everyone gasped and wheezed.

When he was through sneezing, Jonathan asked the man ahead of him, "What was that?"

"The gold escort out of Ballarat. That's how they take the gold down to Melbourne."

Gold? A *whole* cart of it, traveling as fast as possible to keep it safe from bushrangers? It must contain a lot of gold to take such precautions. Jonathan breathed deeply in spite of the dust. Ballarat must be producing a lot of gold indeed!

His father had the same idea. He said, "Johnny, that cart could carry a great deal of gold. I like seeing those soldiers with it. Where soldiers are, there's law and order. I don't think that Ballarat will be like some of the California gold camps, where each man with a pistol thought he was his own law. I haven't seen men with guns hereabouts, and I've liked that."

"Yes, I noticed it too," agreed Jonathan.

Jonathan's second adventure came around noontime, just after they had crossed the slow-moving Columbine River on rafts manned by waiting Australians who extracted a stiff toll from each passenger. The travelers were forced to halt on the crest of a hill and wait for the road below them to empty. Sheep, thousands of them newly shorn of their wool, were crossing to higher grazing grounds. Only two men on horseback and two black-and-white dogs escorted the enormous flock. To Jonathan's great surprise he saw the dogs leap onto the backs of the sheep and run along from back to back, harrying them to greater speed over the road.

Mrs. Manwaren said to Jonathan, "Ah, the sheep are a grand sight when they've got their winter wool! Our blackfellows thought they were clouds when they saw the first sheep we brought here from England. Some tribes still call sheep *jumbucks,* their word for cloud." Suddenly she nudged Jonathan and said, "Ah, yes, I remember. Ye and yer father take no interest in sheep. I see ye be weary. Well, lad, take heart. A bullocky who's been to Ballarat before told my man yesterday that if we go over ten hills on the second day's journey, ye've come to Ballarat. I counted the hills today. Ye've got four more to climb, and then ye'll be there."

# 3

# The Claim on the Creek

After the sheep had passed, Jonathan took up the handles of his now-despised wheelbarrow with a sigh. The blisters they had raised on his palms had broken, leaving red places that oozed and stung. Four more hills to Ballarat? How many miles would that be? How many more hours of pushing the barrow?

Three more hours of toil, noise, and heat brought the travelers at last to the diggings. Jonathan let his barrow drop and stood beside his father to look from the slope of the final hill down onto Ballarat. Words stuck in Jonathan's throat. All he could manage was a broken, "Oh, Pa, is this it?"

Never had he seen a spot so inhospitable as Ballarat. It lay on a plain of dust-brown earth, surrounded by a range of blue, rounded hills. Jonathan's farm-boy eye told him that once this barren plain had been pastureland, but now the grass was gone and only a few tall dusty gums still stood. There was water here. A small, lifeless river with creeks feeding into it glistened yellow-brown in the sun. Below the river to the left, but not flowing into or out of it, was a lake of a bright blue to match the summer sky. This was the only attractive feature here.

And the tents and the people! By the Great Horn Spoon, he'd thought San Francisco and Boston were filled with people, but next to Ballarat they were sparsely settled. Everywhere his eye traveled he saw all shapes and sizes of tents. And there were hundreds and hundreds of people clustered in dark swarms along the banks of the river and creeks, digging, digging, adding to the heaps of piled-up red dirt they already made. Ballarat was crowded as well as ugly beyond belief—the landscape of a bad dream. It was not at all as he'd expected it to be, a place of tall, green trees, cool winds, and swift streams like California had been.

Transfixed by the sight of Ballarat, Jonathan was scarcely aware that the Manwarens were saying farewell to them until his father broke sharply in on him with, "Mind your manners, son. Our friends are leaving us at the bottom of the hill. Say good-bye and thank you to them."

Jonathan looked at the couple he had come to like. He said with a nod, "Thank you for telling me about Australia. Good-bye."

"Good-bye, my dear," came from Mrs. Manwaren, who touched him on the cheek. "I wish ye good fortune here."

"So do I," said her husband. "I hope for yer sake, Mr.

Cole, that ye will have yer shops in California soon. I wish ye sucess in yer digging here."

Charlie Cole, eager to be off downhill, boomed, "Thank you, sir. Thank you! Come, Johnny, let's go down to Ballarat."

After separating from the Manwarens, who led their donkeys onto a trail to the left, Charlie Cole spoke to Jonathan. "Now, don't you go and lose heart. I bet you think this doesn't look like a pleasant spot to live. I agree with you, but look on the bright side. This is where the big nuggets come from."

Jonathan spoke over the drumming, shimmering sound of tiny cicadas celebrating the heat. "But, Pa, there are so many folks here ahead of us!"

"I grant you that. Yet the very fact that there are so many digging here ought to tell you that they must be finding gold or they would have left. Think, what was the only thing we saw on the road going in the direction away from Ballarat?"

"The gold cart. That was all."

"Well, doesn't that make you feel better? Before it's dark we will have looked over the diggings and found us a spot to file a claim on. We can't just start to dig here, I'm sure."

By now the Coles entered Ballarat, walking in the dust behind a lumbering bullock cart. The camp was noisy. Animals, waiting to be slaughtered, bleated and lowed in pens erected beside the butchers' tents. From the large tents that sold food, mining equipment, and offered the services of blacksmiths came a babble of male voices. Behind all these sounds were those of the diggers—the far-off whir of rockers, the thud of hundreds of picks, and the scraping of shovels. There were shouts and cries, a constant deep hum of men; and over all rode the high, maddening thrum of the cicadas.

With others who had just arrived from Melbourne in their party, the Coles started toward the river, picking their way around the clustered large business tents. As they passed along, Jonathan read the signs painted on the canvas sides. One caught his eye and held it—"Tea–Coffee–Cakes–Reading."

Reading? Was it a library and a café? He had gone to a library in Boston and had been astounded at the number of books it held. Sometimes he liked to read, but no one he'd ever known was the reader his father was. "Look, Pa!" Jonathan pointed at the tent.

Cole glanced and said, "Reading, eh? That's good news. We'll go there. But right now the tents with the flags concern us the most."

Jonathan looked where he pointed and saw two large tents not far from each other. One had "License Tent" painted on its side and a red, white, and blue flag blowing in the gusty wind in front. The flag bore a pattern of X-shaped stripes unfamiliar to Jonathan, who would have given much to see his own country's stars and stripes at that moment. The other tent bore a sign saying "Gold Bought Here," and in front of it flew a scarlet banner.

Charlie Cole called out gaily, "I bet we file our claim in the first tent, and you know what we're going to do in the second one!"

By now they were past these tents and walking through groups of smaller ones interspersed with odd-looking, rounded-top huts made of bark, with blankets hung over their entrances. These huts and tents were the homes of the camp's diggers. Many of the small tents, or humpies, had a dog tied beside them that eyed the Coles as they headed for the river.

At the river Charlie Cole had to make a choice. The banks of the Yarrowee River were crowded with men working feverishly with picks, shovels, and pans. Every foot of the bank seemed to be taken, marked out by sticks into small areas. Cole pointed upstream and Jonathan followed him, pushing his barrow, both of them skirting the many heaps of drying-out soil thrown up by the diggers.

When he was abreast of his father again, Jonathan said, "Pa, the claims sure look little here!"

"I saw that too. They appear to be all the same size. I'd say twelve feet by twelve feet. I've got a fine eye for measurements and distances. I guess that's the amount of land a digger is allowed here. I'll find us a spot on one of the creeks not far from that lake we saw. Being close to fresh water will make our washing easier, huh? Creek water's apt to be dirty."

Fifteen minutes of pushing brought them to a tributary creek west of the Yarrowee that was not crowded with diggers. As they went up its south bank, Charlie Cole said, "Remember what I told you in California about always working upstream, not downstream? That's where the big nuggets are. The little ones get washed down, and it's the big ones we want."

Suddenly somebody hailed them. A youngish, clean-shaven, brown-haired man stopped shoveling dirt to lean on his shovel and call out, "Hey, would you be Americans too?" A good-sized brown-and-white dog frisked about him, barking playfully, pulling at the man's trouser leg.

Both the Coles stopped. The older Cole said, "Yes, sir, we are Americans."

The young man spoke to the dog, "You be quiet, Watchie." The dog obeyed and sat down at the man's side, his tongue lolling. The miner asked, "Where do you come from —California?"

Cole answered him, "Yes, and before that from Massachusetts. What about you?"

"From Oregon City. My name's David Mackay." After the two Coles introduced themselves and shook hands with Mackay, the young man went on, "Eight days ago I was a seaman aboard a ship in Melbourne harbor. When I heard the news of this gold strike, I came right up here. I've been here five days. This animal sort of attached himself to me in Melbourne and came here with me."

Charlie Cole asked, "Have you had any luck here?"

"I got a couple of nuggets the size of small pullet eggs. That's not much gold though."

Jonathan asked, "Mr. Mackay, were you a sailor before you came here?"

"Yes, I was."

"Have you seen anybody from the whaler *Wendover* here?"

The Oregon man chuckled and said, "I saw a whole crew of 'em. They came here to Ballarat, took a look at this garden spot, saw what it would cost to outfit here to dig, and left."

Charlie Cole spoke with pride, "We outfitted fairly

cheaply in Melbourne. Where did the men from the *Wendover* go?"

While digging again the Oregonian said, "To Mount Alexander. There's a gold rush there too. If I don't get me another nugget before nightfall, that's where Watchie and I may be off to in the morning." He looked up. "I dug in California too, and let me tell you the diggings here aren't what they're like back home."

"What do you mean?" asked Cole.

"You'll find out once you've staked your claim at the license tent and met the commissioner. For one thing, the claims here are only twelve feet by twelve feet. That's all the land they'll give you."

Cole said, "That's what I figured they were. That's sure small. Say, are there any other Americans here?"

"No, not many Brother Jonathans as yet, but they'll be coming." And Mackay smiled, turned his back on the Coles, and began to dump dirt into the gold pan on the ground at his feet.

Charlie Cole told Jonathan as they left with their barrows, "Now there's a fine young fellow, a credit to America."

A moment after they set out, Mackay's dog came trotting after them. Jonathan remembered his name. He said softly, "Hey, Watchie." This was a friendly dog if he'd ever seen one, but then so was his master, the man from Oregon City.

Three hundred yards farther upstream Charlie Cole stopped at a spot on the creek bank. There were no diggers or mullocky heaps, piles of dirt from excavations, to show that any digging had gone on here before. It was a fresh claim. Across the creek, which was some eighty feet or so wide, they did have neighbors though. Down in the creek panning stood a gray-bearded man who wore one of the Australian-type hats plaited of some sort of leaf. This man's claim was the only one over the way and directly across from where Charlie Cole had stopped and set down his wheelbarrow.

Jonathan stood by his barrow while his father looked the place over with care. Then he announced that it looked good to him, though Jonathan could not truly tell why he thought so. He watched his father reach into his shirt pocket, take out a cloth tape, pick up two rocks, and from the edge of the creek measure off twelve feet along one side. Then Cole put down a stone, measured along the back of the claim, put down the other stone, and measured down to the water's edge. Later he would tamp down stakes, Jonathan knew, doing this properly as it was done in California.

His father told him now, "You stay here to guard this place so nobody else comes along to claim it. I'm going to the license tent." Then he started off away from the creek.

Jonathan sighed as he looked at the marked-off claim. How very small it was! But if men found huge-sized nuggets on so little ground, Ballarat must be mighty rich. He supposed they would pitch their tent on this square too. And that would make it even smaller. He knew that the tent would go near the gum tree stump. That would be a good stool. He went over to it, sat down, and let his eyes wander wearily up and down the banks of the creek, wondering if it had a name.

A splashing sound from across the water made him look to the opposite bank. There he saw a very strange sight. An enormous man had come down into the water with a gold pan to work beside the gray-bearded one. The newcomer wore a most peculiar black hat draped with a veil such as widows wear.

But why would a man wear a veil?

Jonathan got up off the stump and came down to the water's edge to stare. Watchie, who had sat down beside him, got up to follow him. Jonathan and the dog stood there for some time until the gray-bearded miner looked up and saw them. He turned his head and spoke to his veiled partner, who looked up also. At the same moment he looked up, a large, fawn-colored dog appeared and he too remained facing the Cole claim. Then he barked, a deep rumbling growl.

Watchie gave a joyful yelp, followed by a challenging growl, and an instant later flung himself into the water and was swimming to the other side. Jonathan stood looking on, as Watchie breasted the slow current of the dirty stream. Watching the dog swimming, his head high out of the water, made Jonathan smile; but his smile vanished when the other dog splashed down suddenly from the other side of the creek when Watchie was halfway up the bank.

The animals met near the men. There commenced a dog fight such as Jonathan, who had witnessed many dog fights, had never seen or heard. It was the loudest ever—filled with barking, yelping, thrashing, and splashing in the shallows.

Alarmed at the prospect of Watchie getting hurt, Jonathan went down into the stream calling, "Watchie! Watchie, come here!"

Watchie didn't obey him, or in all the noise didn't hear

him. He went on fighting, rolling about with the fawn-colored dog until the gray-bearded man waded forward, gripped Watchie by his collar, lifted him entirely out of the water, and hurled him out in an arc into the middle of the creek. At the same time the veiled man caught hold of his own dog and pushed him momentarily under the water.

Now the gray-bearded man bellowed, "You, boyo, keep yer bedamned dog off me claim!"

Standing in the water, Jonathan shouted, "He doesn't belong to me. He belongs to somebody else, mister."

"I don't care who he belongs to. Keep him away from us and our dog. Keep him off our claim, and keep off it yerself. If the dog comes over to us agin, we'll kill it. If ye come over, boyo, I'll do to ye what I did to this dog just now!"

Kill the dog? Throw Jonathan himself into the creek if he could? Those were strong threats indeed! Fierce anger surged up in Jonathan, but all the same he went back up onto his side of the creek. He looked Watchie over when he came out of the water, but the dog was no worse for his adventure.

Hoping he would obey this time, Jonathan told him, "Go home, Watchie! Go home!" And he made shooing gestures and pointed downstream.

Watchie gave Jonathan a glance, shook himself again, and looked over the water where the fawn-colored dog stood guard on the bank. Mackay's dog barked defiance and received a deep bark in return that seemed to satisfy him. Then he turned his tail to Jonathan and trotted off downstream. An instant later he was chasing a currawong that had swooped low to peck him on his head.

Jonathan went back to his stump, sat down, and kept a

wary eye on the claim over the creek. Judging from the gray-bearded man's accent, he wasn't an Australian. Where had this man come from? And what about the veiled man? Watching him, Jonathan suddenly shuddered. What would make a man cover his face in this heat, where it was hard enough to keep breathing without any covering? While he brushed away flies that tried to rest on him, Jonathan pondered the mystery.

When Charlie Cole returned, Jonathan saw at once that some of his father's earlier jauntiness was gone. He said sharply, "Come on, let's get our tent up before it gets too late. Here the authorities fire a gun at sunset and all digging has to stop for the night. I want to get in some panning before then. I'll tell you how things went at the license tent while we work." As he spoke, he was unloading their tent from the wheelbarrow.

While Jonathan helped him unfold the canvas, Cole went on, "It's like Mackay said. Things are sure different here. I have to pay thirty shillings a month for a license to dig. If I don't pay, the authorities will take back my claim. Troopers will come to get me, hold me in a jail, and then tell me to get out of Ballarat for good."

As Jonathan unwound the thin rope that would be used to steady the tent, his father continued. "Thirty shillings is a lot of money. In Massachusetts a man works in a mill for three days to earn that. I took a look at the price of goods here too. Everything's higher than a cat's back." Suddenly he shrugged. "But men seem to find enough gold here to pay the digging fee. So I filed my claim and heard a lecture on my always respecting the laws of the state of Victoria and of the queen of England. I was told that I, as an American, was not to indulge in talk of republicanism because men here would not be pleased to hear me. I agreed, naturally. Frankly, though, I didn't like being told such a thing. Even if I don't hold with royalty, I would never say so in a land ruled by a queen where we are guests."

Jonathan nodded. Pa was right. "Did you get the idea that they don't like Americans here?"

"No, not really. I think all foreigners get the same lecture if they understand English at all. Ballarat is full of them. I heard a lot of foreign talk on the way to and from the license tent."

Jonathan let the rope fall and now told his father what happened while he was gone. After some thinking, Cole said, "It's not a good start here, is it? But then a bad one often makes for a good ending. I think we'd best be wary of our new neighbors over there. We'll keep to our side of the water, and we'll discourage visits from Watchie."

"Pa, turn your head and look over there now. One of the men's wearing a veil."

"A veil?" Cole swung round, looked for a moment, then said, "Now that is odd! It seems he wants to hide his face. Oh, well, nobody's been hurt. Let's get the tent up, and we'll put our gear into it later."

Working together, the Coles had the tent erected around a telescoping metal pole and the ropes attached and fastened to the ground with stakes in twenty minutes' time. When they were done, Charlie Cole stepped back and looked at it with satisfaction. Then he went to the barrow that had the gold pans packed on it, took them out, and handed one to

Jonathan. How his eyes sparkled and how flushed his cheeks were as he pointed toward the creek. His spirits had revived at the thought of trying their luck here.

Together the Coles waded down into the sun-warmed water and at once began the slow process of panning for gold. Jonathan had never liked panning, but this was a new goldfield and therefore very exciting to him. As he filled his pan a little more than half full with soil from the creek bank, he thought of the nugget he had seen in the Melbourne window. Though he probably would not find one so large in his pan, he could find good-sized ones, if he was lucky. If Dame Fortune smiled?

Now Jonathan sank his pan underwater and began with great care to move its contents about with one hand, washing away what was lightest with the constant flow of creek water. A glance out of the corner of his eye showed that his father was doing the same thing. They both brought their pans toward the surface, swished them around, and tilted them skillfully to let the creek water carry off mud and sand until only the heaviest material remained in the bottoms of their pans. Charlie and Jonathan Cole lifted up their pans within seconds of each other and looked down into them. Nothing! There was nothing in Jonathan's pan but a layer of reddish sand. Sighing, he dumped its contents into the creek and looked disappointedly at his father.

"Johnny, Johnny!" came his father's hoarse, excited whisper. "Come here, son!"

Jonathan waded over to him and looked where he pointed. There on the bottom of his pan lay a gold nugget the size of his little fingernail, shining yellow and beautiful in the late afternoon sunshine. His father said, "I did it! I did it on the first day, on the first try!" Throwing back his head, he cried, "*Eureka!*"

Jonathan watched Cole take the nugget from the pan and turn it in his fingers, admiring it from every angle. "Would you just look at that, Johnny?"

"It's a beauty, Pa. I'll see now if I can get one like it."

As Jonathan bent to refill his pan, he heard a loud booming sound that startled him. What could it be? The men over the creek doing something?

A glance over the water showed him that their neighbors had come up out of the stream. They were walking along the top of the bank together. How strangely they walked, each throwing out one leg to the left, then the other to the right. Jonathan shuddered as he watched them. How large they both were!

"Johnny, that was the sunset gun, remember?" came his father's voice. "That means we have to stop panning until tomorrow. It's the law here."

# 4

## Molly'O

Jonathan lay that night on his blankets, thinking and listening to mosquitoes, the barking of camp dogs, and to the slow gurglings of the nearby creek and of his own stomach. Supper had been only hardtack, leathery dried fruit, and coffee. The boy thought hard about the behavior of the strange pair over the creek and before long he came to a conclusion about them. He decided that they probably resented the Coles filing a claim across from theirs. They'd wanted the creek all to themselves. Perhaps they'd thought to break the law and come over to work the opposite bank and have a double chance of getting rich. By filing where they had, the Coles had put a stop to any such ideas. There had been miners aplenty in California who cursed any man who started to dig

near them. Armed men had watched jealously there to see
that any newcomers never encroached on their claims. Pa
said human nature was pretty much the same the world
over. Why should it be different here?

All at once, Charlie Cole, lying near him, interrupted his
son's thoughts by saying, "I'm going to send you to one of
the butchers' tents tomorrow morning after we pan a bit
together. I want you to buy us some beef for supper tomorrow and a decent breakfast the next morning."

"That sounds good to me, Pa, but first we'll pan, huh?"

"Sure, son. You want to get a nice nugget too, eh? Well,
that's why we came here, isn't it?"

As he came down into the water the next morning, Jonathan looked over the creek. Their neighbors were at work
too, though it was just daybreak. They were working hard,
their eyes on their pans, not on the Coles. That was good!

Later in the morning Dame Fortune favored him. In the
fifth pan he washed out, he found two pea-sized nuggets. He
stifled a shout of joy because he didn't want the men opposite to know he had found something. This was a good
claim, indeed! He waded over and silently showed his pan
to his father, who grinned and pocketed the nuggets for
safekeeping.

Halfway through the morning, just before Jonathan was
to leave to buy the meat, the Coles had a visitor, or rather
two of them. The pleasant young American they had met
the day before came walking along the bank, smiling. He
wore a straw hat with a ribbon dangling down behind. At
his heels trotted the dog, Watchie. Jonathan stared at the

dog, then over the creek; but the men were busily panning and the fawn-colored dog was not in sight.

David Mackay asked, "How do things go with you? Are you finding anything interesting?"

Charlie Cole, followed by Jonathan, waded ashore to say, "We're doing all right. A bit here and there."

"Good." The young man squatted at the brink of the water and said softly, "Don't noise about what you've found. The commissioner keeps good order here and there's no claim jumping that I know of, but all the same there are some mighty rough characters around." He pulled Watchie close to him, began to fondle him, and went on, "I refer of course to convicts." He nodded toward the opposite bank. "Those two over there are old lags. That's what released convicts are called here in Australia. Even if I hadn't been told about them, I'd know they were by the way they walk. Anybody would. They've worn leg-irons."

"Do you know them personally?" asked Charlie Cole.

"No, but I know of them. A bullocky told me. They are Irishmen by birth. As for being convicts, someone in Melbourne pointed out to me how old lags walk. Once you see it, you don't forget it."

Jonathan nodded and asked, "Why does one wear a veil?"

"I don't know. I asked the bullocky that. I've seen the veiled man too. No one has ever seen his face or so the bullocky says."

"Well, they sure aren't freindly," volunteered Jonathan. Now he told his countryman about the fight Watchie and the old lags' dog had had and how the gray-bearded man had threatened the dog and himself.

The American chuckled and said, "Don't take what they say to heart. My dog's not hurt. Probably they don't fancy neighbors. Old lags are often a rough sort who keep to themselves by choice. Such men would call anybody anything."

Charlie Cole nodded. "Yes, there were desperate characters like that aplenty in California."

Mackay rose, stretched, and said, "Well, I'll go back to my claim now. I found some grains of gold this morning, so I reckon I'll stay here for a time. Sometimes I leave my claim and walk about to rest my back."

Cole told him, "I know about that. Panning's hard on a man's back and hands." He added, "I have to send Jonathan for fresh meat now. Who's the best butcher around?"

"He might try Fletcher. He's got a big tent on tent row." Mackay laughed. "Whatever you get will cost you plenty and be tough as leather." He added, looking down at Watchie, "You'd be smart to get yourself a dog if you can to watch your claim at night and when you're both away." Now he jerked his head toward the opposite side of the creek, grinned, and, turning on his heel, headed downstream. Clearly he had meant to warn them of their neighbors.

Cole asked Jonathan, "Do you think you could try to get a dog today too?"

A dog? Jonathan's heart swelled with joy. What a wondrous morning this had been—first his nuggets, then the visit with Mr. Mackay, and now a dog. He had had a liverspotted, flop-eared dog in Massachusetts. He had accompanied Jonathan to school and been ready to fight any dog or bully who attacked him along the way. A dog would be a mighty fine thing to have here.

"Sure, I'll try to get us a dog too."

"All right. Go on to the butcher's now, Johnny. Here's five shillings. See what you can do about a big piece of beefsteak and a dog." Cole smiled. "Don't feed the dog the meat, mind you."

Five minutes later, jingling five silver shillings in his trouser pockets, Jonathan was on his solitary way into Ballarat. He left the Cole claim happy. Delighted to be rid of the cumbersome wheelbarrow, he retraced yesterday's steps past the gold buyer's tent; then the license tent, where a blue-coated trooper stood guard with a carbine; and approached the long, double row of commercial tents. He paused for a moment, looking at the crowd of people rushing down the row, hurriedly entering and hurriedly leaving the tents. Yes, they had that wild, glazed-eyed look he'd seen before as they talked and gestured. It was the California look—the look of gold fever. They left their claims only to buy supplies and conduct any necessary business. The moment they were through they would rush back to dig again. Well, let them do as they pleased.

What he had to do now was buy the meat and then look for a dog. Where would a person buy one in Ballarat? He hadn't seen any tent with "Dogs for Sale" painted on its canvas.

Jonathan had no trouble locating the butcher's tent, where carcasses of cattle and sheep were hanging. He went inside and found two people at work there, a dark-haired man and a tall boy who much resembled the butcher. Both were busy attending to the line of customers. When it was Jonathan's turn to be served, he asked the man for two pounds of beefsteak.

The butcher, a surly man, told him, "That will be one shilling, ha'penny, and when ye come here again, fetch something with ye to carry the meat away in. This time I'll give it to ye in a newspaper. Next time I won't."

Jonathan took out silver coins. His father showed him which were shillings, but what was a ha'penny? Let the man make the change for him.

It was the boy who took Jonathan's two shillings. The butcher had already turned his attention to a miner who couldn't speak English; the man was pointing and gesturing at a hanging carcass of a lamb. Behind him two more customers were waiting to be served.

The boy looked at the coins Jonathan offered, gave him a measuring glance, smiled, and then reached behind him into a tin box. From it he gave Jonathan some coins along with the newspaper-wrapped parcel of meat.

As Jonathan took the package and the coins, the man directly behind him said softly in an accent much like the Manwarens, "Lad, you've been cheated. He owes you more."

Jonathan looked at the coins. Had he been short-changed? That must be what the man meant. Jonathan didn't pocket the change. He shoved out his hand with the coins still in it and asked the boy, "Do you owe me some more?"

He saw the butcher boy's black glance at the Australian miner who'd warned Jonathan and in that moment knew he had been cheated. The boy whirled around and plucked another coin out of the tin box; but instead of giving it to Jonathan, he threw it outside the tent into the dust. He said, "Pick it up if ye want it, new chum!"

Jonathan glared at him in fury. He told him, "You owe it to me. You go out and pick it up and bring it to me."

The boy grinned, slipped out from behind the meat-cutting table into the roadway, and picked up the coin. Holding it high, he taunted Jonathan, "Come and take it!"

Jonathan knew what was coming. He wasn't about to shirk it for an instant either. Out he came, set the meat down, and assumed the posture to fight. He caught the coin the boy threw, stuffed it into his pocket, and took the boy's first blow on his shoulder.

The Australian boy was not only a good fighter but taller and with the longer reach. For every blow Jonathan gave him, he gave back two. One of his punches hit Jonathan directly on the nose, starting it bleeding.

Because of the heat and fury of the fight, Jonathan was only dimly aware that a crowd had gathered in a circle around the two of them. Over the thud of their fists he'd sometimes hear their crying, betting on the shorter or the taller lad. The blow to his nose didn't bring about the finish of the fight, for Jonathan was as willing as ever to go on once the fight had begun.

Suddenly, a thick arm reached among the brawling boys, and at its other end was a trooper, a huge man wearing a visored blue cap. He held the two boys by their shirt collars, shaking each and demanding, "Wot's this? Wot's this now?"

Jonathan wiped away blood and sputtered, "He tried to short-change me."

The trooper released both boys and said, "Well, I've heard that before." He told the other boy, "If I hear that about ye agin, I'll take ye to the commissioner and he'll see what's wot."

Wiping his nose on his sleeve, Jonathan eyed the Australian boy. When he saw him start for the butcher's tent, he bent down and got the parcel.

As he straightened up with it, he looked up into the face of the same gray-bearded man who had yelled at him the day before. The old lag stood, a flour sack on one broad shoulder, looking appraisingly at him. Though other onlookers were grinning, having enjoyed the fight, this man's pale blue eyes were grave.

He told Jonathan something he did not understand at the time. "Well, boyo, I'd say ye did not win the barney, and ye put some men of Ballarat, who don't deserve it, in yer debt for the show ye just now gave 'em. Good day to all here."

"Good day to ye, Delehanty," said the trooper.

Jonathan looked at the man called Delehanty, who now turned about and started off with his strange, swinging stride.

The big trooper towered over Jonathan, shaking his head, then said, "Ah, Yankee, the butcher's son had the better of ye today." Suddenly, he raised his voice to shout, "Molly 'O, come out of yer tent and tend to the bleedin' of this boyo! Molly 'O!"

"Leave off yer shoutin'. Leave off, I say," came a female voice, and a large woman with streaming red hair came pushing through the crowd of men. She stared at Jonathan out of large dark eyes, took off the white apron she wore, and shoved it against his still-bleeding nose. Then she whirled to face the trooper and the others, stamped her foot, and cried, "Why is it ye always call me when there's bloody work to be done? Do ye think I have naught better to do than to tend to yer needs?"

"Ah, see to the lad," shouted a digger. " 'Tis known ye be the one to minister to us all."

"Aye, 'tis known ye be the camp angel," said the trooper, laughing.

While Jonathan's nose trickled onto the cloth of her apron, the woman flared, "If it's common knowledge, ye would know it, O'Connell. Now all of you men go about yer business. Come with me, lad." And she propelled Jonathan ahead of her toward her tent. To his joy it was the very same one with the enticing sign of cakes and reading painted on its side.

A man shouted after them, "Give him a noggin of the Knocker of Ballarat, Molly me love."

"I'd sooner give ye one in yer ear. Come along, lad. Come in and seat yerself, and I'll see to yer nose."

The inside of the tent baffled Jonathan. Looking around, he saw no books, no tea or coffee pots, and, what was far worse, no cakes. There was nothing here but two large tables with benches and stools set beside them, and another table covered with small wooden kegs, a stack of tin cups, and some large earthenware bowls. Perhaps this lady baked in the smaller tent set behind this one?

Jonathan sat down on a stool and, through the apron, he pinched his nose with his fingers to stop the bleeding. He'd done that in other fights, and it had worked just fine. He said, "After a while it'll stop by itself, ma'am. Thank you for the use of your apron. Me and my pa just got here yesterday. We're Brother Jonathans, Americans. I'm sorry to be a bother to you, but the soldier made me come here. I'll go away as soon as he does."

"No, ye will stay here with me!" She sat down beside him and asked, "Tell me why ye were fightin' the butcher's lad."

"Because he didn't give me the change I was supposed to get. I don't know the money here yet."

"Ah, so that was it? That lad's been accused of that before."

"And he's guilty too!"

The woman said, "Ye had best learn the money here as quickly as ye can. Not all are honest in Ballarat."

"They aren't in California either, ma'am. Or at least that's what Pa says."

Jonathan took the apron from his nose, looked into it, and saw that his nose still bled a little. He put it back and asked in a muffled voice, "Are you Irish, ma'am?"

"Aye, from Dublin Town eight years past."

Jonathan took down the apron, looked into it again, and found that his nose had stopped bleeding. He put the apron on the tabletop and said, "My pa and I were told that the two men who have the claim across the creek from us are Irishmen, convicts from Van Diemen's Land. We heard that they used to wear iron chains and were very dangerous."

The woman nodded. "Aye, I know who they are. Those two poor souls did wear chains. Both the wild, angry ones and the bolters, those who tried to run away, wore irons on their legs. Such men are best not trifled with even now that they are freed."

Poor souls? Jonathan stifled a laugh, but he did agree that they were best left alone. He asked, "Ma'am, do you know why one of the men over there has a veil over his face? My pa and I wonder about that."

"Och, Liam? I've never seen Liam's face. No one has ever said he has. Michael Delehanty, his mate, comes here some-times, but never Liam. Perhaps he cannot drink without his face bein' seen, and he wants none to see it. I do not know."

Jonathan, who had understood little of this, changed the subject to ask, "Where do you make the coffee and tea and bake your cakes; and where are your books, please?"

"Cake? 'Tis cake ye want?" Her eyes widened, then she shouted with laughter. "Cakes? I've got no cakes. I've not no coffee and no tea. What do ye think I sell here, boyo?"

"I don't know, ma'am."

Chuckling now, the big woman patted Jonathan on the arm. "This is naught but a grog shop." She gestured toward the kegs. "I sell gin, rum, beer, and brandy. Because as yet I have no license to sell drink, I must say that I sell coffee and tea, which need no license here. Some other tents ye see that offer tea and coffee are also grog shops. Only a green new chum would not be knowin' that."

"My pa don't know either."

She nodded, then said, "Ah, America must be very differ-ent. Bring him in to see for himself." She winked, "I'll have lemonade for ye."

"Sure, we'll come, ma'am. My name's Jonathan Cole. Thank you for the use of your apron. I ought to wash the blood out of it for you, but right now I don't know where to." Then he asked, remembering, "Ma'am, where can I go to buy a watchdog?"

She stood up. "From meself. At the moment I've got three dogs where one will do. They've been gifts to me from men soon done with their diggin' here, not willin' to bend their backs workin' as hard as they must after gold. I've got a black one I'll sell ye for a shillin'. He'll keep watch for ye well enough." She smiled and asked, "Would ye be afraid of Delehanty and Liam, yer neighbors over the creek?"

Jonathan flushed and lied to her, saying, "No, of course not. Somebody told us to get a dog, that's all. Pa and me, we dug in California where it's plenty wild. We weren't scared where lots of men wear pistols."

She laughed. "No, ye're a brave one. I see that ye stand up and fight even if ye haven't got yer height yet. How old are ye, ten or eleven?"

Jonathan sighed. "No, I'm thirteen. Yes'm, I'll fight. I have to. I always fight when boys call me a runt." He grinned at her, pointing to the empty space among his front teeth. "A boy in San Francisco knocked that out."

Folding her arms, she asked, "And what did ye do to him?"

"Blacked both of his eyes."

She was smiling. "Did ye now?"

"I sure did." Jonathan warmed to her. He asked, "Should we be extra careful around folks here who've been convicts?"

"Common courtesy and no pryin' is all any one of us who's been transported as a convict ever asks. 'Tis all I ask of any man or boy."

Jonathan sucked in his breath. What had he said? This lady had been a convict too! He felt the red heat of embarrassment creeping up his neck to his face. Snatching at a different subject, he asked, "Should we be extra careful of the troopers and the commissioner?"

Her smile had gone now. "Aye, be wary of them all. They could come burn me out because I have no license if I was not protected. They know that I permit no fighting, never a barney here, and I will make no trouble for them. Now, wait here, and I'll fetch ye a dog who needs a master." And she was gone.

A moment later she was back with a large, curly-haired black dog with a rope around his neck. The delighted Jonathan grinned at the animal and gave her a shilling, thinking that this was a very handsome dog. He said, "The dog comes cheaper than beefsteak does. Thank you, ma'am, for everything. I'll come back. Thank you for answering all my questions."

"Don't people reply to all ye ask?"

"Not always, but my pa generally tries to. Pa and I are alone; my mother's dead. Sometimes though Pa has his mind on other things. He's got a lot of ideas about how he would like things to be when we go back to America. He's going to be disappointed that you haven't got books and journals in here. He likes them. He wanted to come here and read."

"And ye had hoped to come here and eat cakes? Well, why not? I once knew another lad who liked cakes too."

"We'll both come here though and drink some of your lemonade."

She chuckled and said, "Men don't drink lemonade in Ballarat."

"I'll tell Pa that."

Hauling the dog with him, Jonathan went to the tent opening and stuck his head out. A sweeping glance told him that no one was laying in wait for him outside. He gave a little jerk to the dog's rope and, carrying the meat under one arm, stepped outside into the heat and winds of midday.

How his nose stung from the blow it had received! His shirt front was dark with drying blood, and his entire body ached from the punches he'd got from the butcher's boy.

Jonathan stopped to look at the dog. He patted him and the animal moved nearer to him. This dog was surely worth more than a shilling. How fine and large he was. Jonathan preferred large dogs to small ones. Who wouldn't?

Jonathan said lovingly, "We'll be real good friends, won't we?"

The dog tilted his head to one side and looked up at the boy as if he understood. Jonathan put his arm around the animal's neck, hugged him, and said, "I'm going to name you right now. I'm going to call you Joker after the dog I had in Massachusetts. Would you like to be named that? We were Jonathan and Joker to everybody who knew us. Joker was a real good dog. I hated to leave him with my aunt when we went to California. He'd follow me everywhere I went. We were a real pair. Folks said I should have named him Shadow."

Jonathan looked at the rope around the dog's neck, thinking that the other Joker hadn't needed a collar or a leash. He told the black dog, "I bet you don't need that rope, do you? You'd follow me without it, wouldn't you, Joker?"

He untied the rope and stood beside the dog, who had just

sat down to scratch behind his ear. Jonathan took a step forward, whistled softly, and said, "Let's go. Come on, Joker."

The black dog started off but to Jonathan's dismay not behind him at a walk but away at a bounding run. He ran, ears flopping, barking, always ahead of Jonathan. The boy ran after him calling, "Joker, Joker," but the dog did not stop. Joker ran as if he knew where he wanted to go. Perspiring heavily, Jonathan ran after him in the heat, angry at himself for letting him off the rope before he really got to know the dog. The only good thing was that he was running in the direction of the Coles' claim. But would he never stop?

Stop though Joker did at last. He slowed to a trot, then to a walk, and finally hunkered down at the edge of the blue waters of little Lake Wendouree. There he lay on his belly drinking thirstily while Jonathan came stumbling up to him, sweat running into his eyes. He reached down and tied the rope to the dog's neck, then stood up to let him finish drinking. He must have been very thirsty; that could explain his running off.

As Joker lapped noisily at the water, Jonathan gazed out over the lake, thinking how cool it looked. Then he stared at his own shirt front. A moment later he set down the meat. Shifting the dog's rope from hand to hand, he took off his shirt. After the shirt came his boots and stockings. Why not wade in the clear, fresh water while he laundered his shirt? He felt dry as an old bone from the long journey from Melbourne.

Jonathan waited until Joker had done drinking, then he

77

tied the dog's rope to his own waist. He was not going to take any chances trusting Joker with the meat. Perhaps he and Pa would come here to swim after supper tonight. Pa fancied swimming.

His shirt in one hand, Jonathan started for the water's edge but halted at the strange hissing noise he heard coming from behind him to the right. What was it, a snake?

Jonathan spun around to locate it. There, standing under a tall gum, were three black natives. These weren't like the ones he had seen leaving Melbourne. They had been dressed in a combination of rags and finery; but these three, a boy and two tall but spindly men, wore nothing but loincloths, with rags tied at their shoulders. All three carried long spears; all three were hissing.

Jonathan froze, waiting for Joker to growl; but no sound came from the dog as the native boy limped forward, his hand outstretched. When he was near Jonathan, he smiled, also showing a tooth missing in front of his mouth. He said one word only, "Tucker?"

Jonathan stared at him and at his motionless adult companions. Was Tucker the native boy's name? No, it couldn't be. He'd clearly said it as a question.

Eyeing the spear, Jonathan glanced about swiftly to see if any help was nearby. No, he and the black fellows were alone. No one was looking their way.

Now the native boy repeated, "Tucker? Tucker?" He pointed to the dog and said, "Molly?"

Molly? Ah, he knew the dog and the lady who kept the grog tent. No wonder Joker hadn't growled at him. Jonathan thought he knew what the boy was asking him—if his name were Tucker.

He pointed to himself. "No, I'm not Tucker. I'm Cole. Jonathan Cole. Who would you be?"

There was no reply, only the repeated word, "Tucker?"

"No, no, no Tucker." Jonathan shook his head. At the same time he started toward the lake, passing the native lad.

Suddenly the shaft of the boy's spear barred his way, pushing him firmly back from the water.

Jonathan stepped backward to face the young aborigine, who was scowling and shaking his head. With the spear shaft he shoved Jonathan back toward his boots and stockings until he stood beside them. Now the other boy shifted the spear to hold it upright. He limped to the lake's edge, knelt down, and shoved his left arm up to the shoulder into the water, making it swirl about his arm. After a short time he withdrew his arm, got up, and came over to Jonathan to display it. Four big brown leeches had fastened themselves to his flesh. The lovely lake must be alive with the horrible things, and Jonathan had been about to wade in it! He stood transfixed with horror as the black boy pulled the sucking leeches from his arm and let them fall into the dust to die.

"Thank you. Thank you," came from Jonathan, who wanted only to put on his boots and stockings and get away from the lake, as well as from the black men.

"Tucker?" asked the native boy.

That again? Jonathan sighed. Well, he'd put a stop to that forever now. He pointed to himself and shouted, "Cole! Jonathan Cole." He caught hold of the boy's hand and shook it, saying Cole over and over again, pointing to himself, smiling at the native as if to show his friendliness.

The grinning aborigine pumped his hand, smiling too; then he called out something in his own language that made the two men come forward. Now the boy pointed to his own missing tooth, to Jonathan's missing tooth, then to the adult blackfellows who were looking surprised at Jonathan. Suddenly they also smiled and pointed to their own mouths. They too lacked the exact same front tooth.

The aborigine boy hit his chest with his small fist and said, "Prince Billy."

"Jonathan Cole," said Jonathan, glad to be understood at last. He added happily, "No tucker."

"No tucker," repeated one of the men, who then turned around and started off with the other following him. The boy was last to go. He looked gravely at Jonathan, at the writhing leeches, at the dog, at the boots and stockings, and finally at the parcel of meat. Then he limped away also and left Jonathan to put on his clothing.

# 5

## Prince Billy

Charlie Cole's first words to him back at the claim minutes later were, "I see you got us a dog."

"Yes, I called him Joker. I sure got a lot to tell you, Pa." Jonathan looked over the creek. Yes, Delehanty was there; but he was busily at work, not looking in this direction. The veiled man was nowhere to be seen.

Cole said quietly, "Johnny, I see by your shirt that you've been fighting again. Did you start it?"

"No, Pa." Kneeling at the edge of the creek, speaking softly, Jonathan told of all the morning's events.

Cole said thoughtfully after he turned to look at the old lag over the stream, "Well, it seems Mr. Mackay picked the wrong butcher, eh? We won't go back to that one again. I'm glad, though, somebody told you what the boy was up to and you got our money back. There are some nice folks here besides Mr. Mackay and the lady who helped you. This is a good claim. I don't intend to be run off it. If our neighbors or anybody else gives us trouble, I'll go to the commissioner with a complaint. Now why on earth do you suppose that native boy did what he did saving you from the leeches?"

"I don't know."

"I suspect you may never find out either. But you say you liked the woman at the grog tent?"

"Yes, she wants to meet you too."

"Does she? I think I'd like to make her acquaintance too and thank her for her friendship to you. Now tie Joker up so he won't run off again and get the other gold pan. Let's see how well you do panning this afternoon. You can wash your shirt later. After all, you don't want to lose any more of the daylight, do you?"

Jonathan panned the remainder of the day, gathering only some grains of gold. While he did the monotonous work he knew so well, he thought of the native boy who had saved him from the lake and of Molly. If the boy knew the black dog, he knew Molly, of course. What was Molly to the blackfellow? This was a strange, threatening land, not easily understood. And as their fellow American, the pleasant David Mackay, had rightly said, the gold camp of Ballarat wasn't at all like the diggings of California!

That evening Mackay came strolling to the Coles' camp, bringing them a gift. It was a board that would serve as a tabletop when placed on two kegs. He apologized for its being warped, saying, "Timber's hard to come by here. A lot of Australian wood, I'm told, doesn't cut straight or is too soft or too hard to cut at all. I've got the other end of this board."

Charlie Cole thanked Mackay, then invited him to have coffee with them. Mackay was given the place of honor on the stump, while the two Coles sat on the ground. After listening to them tell about their day, Mackay talked about himself, of Oregon City, of digging in several camps in California, and of the schooner that had brought him to Melbourne from China. Mackay was a man of two trades, sailor and miner, and of the two he preferred mining.

When Jonathan said he liked the sea, Mackay told him, "A man doesn't get rich as an able seaman."

"I think I might like to be a captain of a clipper ship."

"Oh, that's a real ambition now." Mackay laughed and began to talk with Charlie Cole of something else.

While the two men talked, Jonathan listened to the night. Owls were about in the vicinity of the creek. Over the by-now familiar noises of men speaking loudly in the distance, dogs barking, and donkeys braying, he could hear their soft hootings. The constant flies were gone. The cicadas were silent in the cool weather, and only the mosquitoes were about, whining into one of his ears or the other.

Suddenly, he heard singing. It was a clear tenor voice coming from somewhere nearby. Charlie Cole stopped talking and listened too.

*"There was a wild Colonial Boy, Jack Donahue, by name*
*of poor but honest parents he was born in Castlemaine.*
*He was his father's dearest hope, his mother's pride and joy.*
*O fondly did his parents love their Wild Colonial Boy.*

*He was scarcely sixteen years of age when he left his father's home.*
*A convict to Australia, across the seas to roam.*
*They put him in the Iron Gang in the Government employ;*
*but ne'er an iron or earth could hold the Wild Colonial Boy."*

On and on went the haunting, soaring ballad with Jonathan hanging onto every word sung of the life and tragic death of the bold bushranger. As the song ended with Donahue's being shot to death by the horse police, Jonathan felt like applauding the singer. He did not, however, for by now he knew that the singing came from the claim over the creek. But who was the singer, Delehanty or the veiled man?

When the song ended, Charlie Cole said, "What a fine voice! What was that tune, Mackay?"

"I've heard it before. It's often sung here at night. It's called 'The Wild Colonial Boy.' I think it must be to Australia what 'Oh, Susanna' is to our country. It came from over the stream. Hard to believe that one of the old convicts can sing like that, isn't it?" He asked Jonathan, "Well, boy, why don't you sing that tune of ours to entertain your neighbors now?"

Jonathan shifted uncomfortably and said, "I'd better not sing 'Oh, Susanna.' I don't get on too good with those men, remember."

Mackay gave him an approving look and said, "You could be right. Whoever sang it might take it as a challenge to his song. You know, you've got good sense, Johnny Cole."

"Jonathan and I thank you for the compliment," said his father. Then, changing the subject, he now asked, "Why do you dig alone, Mackay?"

"I haven't met anyone so far I'd fancy as a partner. I'll be wanting another American when I do, a Brother Jonathan. I wasn't lucky enough to have a fine son like you, Cole." As the man spoke, Joker came over to him to be petted and to rest his head on Mackay's knee.

Jonathan asked, "Do you know much about the blackfellows here?"

"No, but I can tell you about the tucker mixup you told me about. Tucker is a word used here to mean food. The natives were begging food from you, not asking your name."

"Oh. But why did the boy save me from the leeches?"

"Now that is something I don't know. I know what tucker means only because I've seen those three natives hanging around asking for tucker and being given food by Australian diggers." Removing Joker's head from his knee, he got up to say, "Thanks for the coffee. I think I'll go back to my claim and get some sleep. By the way, in case you've lost track of the days, it's Saturday tomorrow. You advance a day on the calendar coming here from America. There's no work done on Sundays by order of the commissioner."

Cole said, "Thank you for telling us today's Friday; I'd thought it was Thursday. I have lost track of the days. Is there a church here?"

"None that I know about. If you hear of one, let me know. There's a lot to be said for a good uplifting Sunday sermon."

Saturday was the hottest day yet. Jonathan was content to be down in the creek panning, because it was the coolest place he knew. Keeping his back turned to the opposite bank, he filled his pan, washed it out and emptied it, and thought happily of going tonight to Molly's tent. Pa had promised they would go.

During the day Jonathan gave little thought to their neighbors, for one glance had shown him that both were in the creek too, panning with their backs to him and their dog lying on the bank watching everyone. He felt the old convicts would have their sights set today on getting big nuggets before Sunday, not on making any trouble for their Yankee neighbors.

That night as he walked through Ballarat with his father to Molly's grog tent, Jonathan kept an eye peeled for Prince Billy but did not see him. It wasn't until they had strolled past a number of tents that Jonathan spied the native boy. He squatted on his haunches with the men he'd been with before, all three of them in a row outside the smaller of Molly's tents.

Jonathan nudged his father and said, "That's them, Pa. Those are the natives I saw yesterday."

"Well, they surely are more wild-looking than the people we saw in Melbourne," commented Charlie Cole. "Don't stop. We'll go straight on. We haven't got any tucker for them in any event."

As Jonathan had hoped, red-haired Molly made them very welcome. She left a pair of miners drinking at one table to seat the Coles at another; and she at once asked Jonathan, "And how would yer poor nose be now?"

"It doesn't hurt too much. Thank you for asking." Jonathan went on shyly, "This is my pa, Charlie Cole. I'm sorry, ma'am, but I don't know your last name."

"Quinn. 'Tis Molly Quinn, and happy I am to make yer acquaintance, Mr. Cole. I'll fetch ye lemonade, Johnny. What will it be for ye, Mr. Cole—Spider, Fench, stout, or the Knocker of Ballarat, which is ready; or would ye rather have a nobbler of gin or rum?"

Jonathan saw his father flinch and heard him ask, "What is the Knocker of Ballarat, a punch? Or some form of whiskey. Now and then I drink punch."

Recalling what a man watching his fight had called out, Jonathan interrupted, "Mrs. Quinn, that's what a man said you ought to give me, the Knocker of Ballarat."

She laughed and told him, "'Tis not for the young shoots. In truth 'tis a brew for few men. 'Tis rum, red pepper, methyl alcohol, hot water, and opium stirred together and left overnight to ripen."

"Good heavens!" came from a startled Charlie Cole.

"Och, I'll give ye Spider, 'tis only brandy and lemonade."

"That will do splendidly," said Cole.

Mrs. Quinn was back quickly with two tin cups. As she handed one to each of the Coles, Jonathan asked, "Do you know the blackfellows outside here? I think the boy is called Prince Billy. He saved me yesterday from leeches in the lake. I didn't know what he meant when he asked me for tucker."

The woman laughed, then said, "So, they be here again? They come to me for tucker. I'll give them some later tonight. They'll wait for me where they are; they're a patient people. So Prince Billy saved ye, eh? I wager ye wonder why he did that?"

"Yes'm, I do. Would you know why?"

Molly reached out a finger to touch Jonathan's upper lip. "'Tis this. Ye've lost a tooth, and they have had that tooth knocked out to prove them men and hunters. So they think ye to be a man and a hunter like themselves."

"My Jonathan?" exclaimed Cole in disbelief.

"Aye, 'tis a mark of favor to yer lad in their eyes."

Speechless with astonishment, Jonathan could only look into the murkiness of his lemonade. He had felt self-conscious about that lost tooth for weeks. It was hard to believe that a fight in San Francisco could do him some good in Australia, but it had.

Finding his tongue, Jonathan asked, "How much English does Prince Billy know?"

"A few words that I taught the poor lad. I know a bit of his language. I've been told his story by a sheepherder who once came in here. A man with a cart drove over Prince Billy's foot when he was but a babe, a'crawlin' on the ground." She went on, ignoring the Coles' gasps of horror. "He's motherless to boot. His mother and his sisters were given flour laced with poison by a farmer when they came to him to ask for tucker. The farmer thought that other blackfellows of their band had stolen and killed one of his lambs."

"Good Lord!" exploded Charlie Cole. "And I had imagined that the natives were well treated here because they are not slaves! How frightful. That situation should have been remedied at once by law. Who are the men with the boy? Is one his father?"

"I do not know. They are from his band. They reared him."

"Well, well, what a sad tale." Charlie Cole shook his head. Then lifting his cup, he changed the subject, saying, "Your Spider is excellent."

She smiled at him, said, "Thank ye," and then asked, "Did yer lad tell ye I came here to Australia as a convict?"

"Yes, and I am sure that you were innocent of any crime."

"Not a bit of it!" Now she slapped the table and cried, "I was guilty. I took a fine, lace-trimmed petticoat off the washing line of an English judge, and I made sure I was seen as I did it."

As Cole sputtered on a swallow of his drink, she went on, "I take it ye have heard of the famine in Ireland in 1845?"

"Yes, yes, ma'am. It was a very terrible thing. There was a blight on the potato crop, wasn't there?"

"Indeed, sir, a terrible blight that poisoned the potatoes with rot. Thousands fled to America." Mrs. Quinn spoke quietly now, leaning forward. "Thousands starved to death in Ireland, including my own poor lad who was never strong and my man, my husband, who would not steal. I stole in order to be caught, sent to a gaol, and fed there as a prisoner of the English. I wanted to be transported to a place where I might not die. I was sent here and went to work for a tavern keeper in Melbourne. He was a good master, who paid me well and let me put the money by to save it. Because I behaved myself, I was given a ticket-of-leave when my time was up. I came here to make me fortune sellin' grog to diggers." She nodded her head. "Being transported is a common enough tale here among the Irish. I think there is no shame to it much of the time."

Jonathan said, "I think you are very brave."

"I agree with my son," said Cole, who then asked, "When do you expect to return to Ireland?"

"Return? To ask me that ye must be a very new chum. Mr. Cole, I can never go home. That was agreed to when I got my ticket-of-leave. I can go anywhere in the world I choose but never back to Ireland. If I should go home and am caught there, I will be transported here to Australia again."

"I didn't know about tickets-of-leave," said Charlie Cole slowly. "I see there's a good bit to be learned here."

"Indeed there is. I found that out when I first came to Australia too. Well, though I cannot go home, I can dream of Ireland. No one can take my dreams from me."

"Ah, you are correct in that, ma'am. A person must live on his dreams and try to make them come true."

As Cole started to talk about his dreams and plans, some men entered. Molly got up to serve them, then waited at the opening of her tent to greet yet another newcomer. It was Delehanty.

The old convict looked sharply at the Coles but said nothing as he seated himself. He ordered rum and sat alone, drinking it in silence.

By now Jonathan was plenty weary of his neighbor over the creek. He pulled at his father's sleeve and whispered, "Let's go back to our claim."

"Finish your lemonade, son. Remember, we have every bit as much right in here as any other man. When we're done, we'll go. Don't look at him."

Jonathan obeyed, looking everywhere in the tent but at Delehanty.

After a time Molly returned to sit down with Jonathan and his father again. She told them softly and with pride, "That'd be Mr. Michael Delehanty over there. He was a hero, I'm told, in Ireland. He pulled an English soldier off his horse and thrashed him with a stick. That's why he was sent to Van Diemen's Land. He's a famed man in Australia. There's a song sung about him."

"A song?" asked Charlie Cole.

"Aye, a ballad."

Once more Jonathan glanced at Delehanty and found him looking at him through a haze of smoke as he puffed on his pipe. It was as if the man knew he was being discussed. Jonathan did not look his way again.

Molly continued, "I've not heard it sung, but I've been told 'tis about his days when he was a convict in Van Diemen's Land."

"Were murderers transported there?"

The woman shook her head from side to side. "No, highwaymen and murderers were hanged at home, not sent out as convicts. Mr. Delehanty did not kill the English soldier. If he had, he would have hanged in Ireland." Suddenly she changed the topic of conversation, saying, "Now, I'll tell ye what I tell all new chums who come in here. If ye have no calendar, make yerself one so ye'll never miss the date ye must pay for yer new license. The troopers will keep track and come after ye if ye fail to make the payment."

"Thank you, I've been warned about them before," said Charlie Cole, who drained the last of his Spider and got up now.

When the Coles started out, Molly escorted them to the

entrance. Charlie Cole again thanked her for the kindness she had shown to Jonathan and promised to come again.

"And ye will be most welcome," Molly said. "Good luck to ye in yer digging. I hope ye find the yellow dodger all men seek here." She smiled down at Jonathan. "If I do bake a cake, I'll see to it that ye be the first one to know of it."

"Thank you, ma'am. I'll come here right away if you do bake one."

As Jonathan went out with his father into the hot night, he saw that the aborigines were still beside the smaller tent. When the Coles were abreast of him, Prince Billy arose to look directly at Jonathan. The young American nodded and smiled. By the yellow light coming through the cloth of the tent, he could see that the native boy was grinning; and he lifted his hand in what Jonathan considered some sort of greeting.

Jonathan confided very softly to his father, "Pa, I think I've made a friend my own age here."

Cole spoke softly too. "Even if that boy saved you from the leeches, Johnny, I want you to be wary of him. It appears to me that these Australian natives think very strangely. Can you imagine anyone being esteemed for having a tooth missing in a particular place in his mouth? But such a thing seems to bring admiration here."

*Admiration?* Jonathan stopped, pondering the word his father had just used. Yes, that was what he had felt with the three blackfellows—interest in him, curiosity, and admiration for him in spite of his small size. All at once a warm glow enveloped him. He had never been admired by anyone before.

# 6

## The Sandy Blight

Ten days passed with both Coles working hard. Occasionally they found small nuggets, and more often grains of gold showed up in their pans; but there were no more nuggets the size of pullet eggs. After a time of fruitless panning, Jonathan began to reflect on their hard times in California, where they had worked for days at a stretch and got nothing for their toil. He still believed as his father did that there was gold here somewhere; but as he panned doggedly each day finding almost nothing, both his enthusiasm and the memory of the nugget he had seen in Melbourne faded. That thirty shillings-a-month license fee could turn out to be a big worry to them. Ballarat was a mighty expensive place in which to live. Nuggets would have to start showing up fairly often in their pans to keep them going.

The Coles were not disturbed again by the two old lags, though sometimes Jonathan could hear Delehanty's voice over the water. Their only company was David Mackay, who brought his dog with him. Jonathan was worried about how the two dogs would get along. He did not want the Coles' dog to embarrass them in front of their guest. But Watchie got on well with Joker after a few snarls. This was just as well, thought the boy, because Joker would probably lose any fight that took place.

By this time Jonathan had concluded that Joker wasn't much like the previous dog by that name. Although he was handsome and friendly, the dog did not seem to have much sense. Pa said he wondered if Joker barked at all when anyone came onto their claim and neither of them was there. Even worse, Joker was inclined to chew on his rope. Jonathan had to inspect it now and then to see that he didn't get through it entirely and then just wander away.

On the eleventh day the Coles looked up from the creek bed to see the three blackfellows standing on the dusty bank above them, leaning on their spears. Their ragged shoulder coverings fluttered in the hot winds. One of the men pointed to Jonathan, then to his own mouth, and all three natives grinned.

The boy, Prince Billy, limped forward and asked, "Tucker?"

Charlie Cole told Jonathan, with a sigh, "They've come begging. I suppose they do that all over the camp, and now it's their time at our claim."

Jonathan said, "Pa, I owe the boy something, don't I?"

Cole was thoughtful. "Yes, you do. All right, give them

some of the damper you made last night."

"Sure."

Jonathan scrambled up out of the water and went into the tent. He brought out a slab of the hard-as-clay bread he baked the night before, which the Australians called damper. This bread, coffee, and meat were the mainstays of a Ballarat miner's daily diet. David Mackay had shown him how to make it; he baked it on a hot stone one day while they were visiting him. Damper was pretty tasteless but was all right when eaten freshly baked. The next day it was very tough indeed.

"Here's some damper," said Jonathan, giving the disk to Prince Billy. He added, "It's not much good, but it's all there is now."

Prince Billy looked at it, said, "*Kabbin,*" then pointing to Joker said, "*bokka.*"

"Dog," said Jonathan, smiling, nodding, and pointing to Joker.

"Come along, son," called his father, and the boy went back into the creek. The aborigines left with the food moments later.

Cole said, "You did the right thing. When the natives come again, give them damper if there's any left over. There's no point in making them angry, and the boy did help you out."

"Yes, he did, Pa. I was glad we had something to give them."

The next morning, after several hours of panning, Charlie Cole suddenly dumped the contents of his pan into the stream and said disgustedly, "Humbug, Johnny! We're not getting anywhere panning. I'm going to make us a rocker machine. Shoveling dirt into a rocker to separate the gold from the earth can sure speed things up for a prospector. We'll start making one this morning. I'll simply have to pay out the cash for whatever materials we need. I know there's gold here, but I think between us we've cleaned out the creek area. It's time for us to start digging. David Mackay said he was going to make a Long Tom sluice box."

Jonathan only nodded. From his California days he knew what a rocker and a Long Tom were. He had helped build both of the mining machines.

Working together and sweating heavily, the Coles constructed a rocker, a crude machine of wood shaped like a baby's cradle with a bin, or hopper, attached to one end. Wire mesh was nailed over the bin, and canvas cloth with cleats fastened to it lined the bottom. The only good thing about a rocker, so far as Jonathan was concerned, was that mining with it was indeed a faster process than panning. But operating a rocker or a Long Tom, its longer version, was very hard work for two men. While his father dug on the bank, shoveling dirt into the screen-covered bin, Jonathan went back and forth to the creek, filling buckets with water to pour over the dirt. The water washed the finer material down through the mesh onto the canvas. Then the two of them shook the rocker, forcing even more dirt and gravel down, where any gold in the shoveled material would catch on the cleats and be picked up.

How brutal the work was in the fierce heat of midsummer! How dreadful the choking dust their digging stirred up! It made them cough again and again and keep rubbing their eyes. To make matters worse, their clothing stuck to their bodies with sweat, but they dared not remove their shirts because the swarms of stinging insects would at once attack any inch of bare flesh. The flies were a torment, for they came over and over at their eyes, mouths, and noses. No matter how often they were brushed away, an instant later the tiny yellow-brown nuisances returned, landing on their backs, crawling there momentarily, riding on them, then flying to their faces. Charlie Cole's back was dark with them, and Jonathan knew that the back of his shirt was also.

The day after they made their rocker, Jonathan heard hammering from over the creek and saw that the old lags were making one too. After that there was the same grating, *swish-swish* sound from their rocker as from the Coles. At the end of that week it seemed to Jonathan that every man on their creek had a rocker operating too.

By now greener "new chum" diggers had come to file on the properties on both sides of the Coles as well as over the creek. To the right of the Coles were a man and his two tall, yellow-haired, blue-eyed sons; on the other side were two small, dark men with large mustaches. Charlie Cole, ever friendly, tried in vain to talk with their new neighbors. Although they smiled and nodded at the Coles, they knew no English. Cole told Jonathan that he thought the blond family was Dutch or German and the mustached newcomers Italians, but who knew for certain.

The contents of their rocker disappointed the Coles, for they still found no big nuggets. The machine produced more small ones than panning had, and that convinced Charlie Cole all the more that there was gold to be found on their claim.

One day he decided that it was time to bring the gold they

had garnered to the gold buyer's tent. Jonathan went with him. There were other miners in line before them waiting to have their nuggets weighed and exchanged for British coins. Some had been luckier than Jonathan and his father and held more and larger nuggets. The Coles looked at them enviously as these men pocketed golden guineas and silver shillings, for both of them knew they would be given less when their gold was weighed. The amount they did receive deeply disappointed them.

As Charlie Cole was being paid by the gold buyer, Delehanty came pushing into the tent. He stood there, his arms folded, clearly waiting for the Coles to leave before he brought out his gold for weighing.

Charlie Cole told Jonathan, "Come along, son," and the two of them went outside into the hot sunshine and dusty wind that whipped about the red flag in front of the tent.

Jonathan said, "I wonder how those old lags are doing. Delehanty sure didn't want us to see what he had."

His father told him, "That's not any of our affair," and sighed. "I just know there's plenty of gold hereabouts, and some of it's on our claim. I dream at night of finding it! I plan to keep our claim, even if we are finding it hard to pay the license fee each month. I have a feeling it's a good claim! My hunch says to stay with it."

Jonathan said nothing, because just at that moment he spied Mrs. Quinn coming toward them, a basket over her arm. Behind her, also carrying a basket, came Prince Billy.

"Pa, let's go talk to the lady," cried Jonathan, who didn't want to hang about the gold buyer's tent with Delehanty due to come out any minute.

The Coles went up to Molly Quinn and both doffed their

hats. In return they received a "Good day to ye," a curtsey, and a smile. She told them, "I'm bound to the butcher's. Prince Billy is helping me fetch and carry before he and the others go walkabout later today. He tells me he is going."

"Go walkabout?" asked Charlie Cole.

"Go a'wandering, sir. The blackfellows do that when the spirit moves them to wander."

"Yes, some of our Indian tribes do that too. They are nomads."

Jonathan looked with envy at the aborigine boy, thinking that he himself must go back to the creek and the rocker, the things that were his world in Ballarat. All day long he would sweat in the heat; smell dirty, brown creek water; be assailed by noise and insects and suffer from dust blown into his face. He looked around at what he could see of the plain of Ballarat between the tents. What terrible things had been done here to the land in the name of gold. If there wasn't riches here, no one would stay for a moment. Prince Billy and the men of his band would wander green, cool places like those the Coles had traveled past on their way to Ballarat. Though the blackfellows sometimes begged, they were freer than he was; they were not fettered to gold.

As Mrs. Quinn and Charlie Cole stood talking, Delehanty came out of the tent, pocketing the money he'd just received.

Mrs. Quinn saw him and said, "Good day to ye, Mr. Delehanty." She sank down into a curtsey deeper than the one she had given the Coles. It was clear to Jonathan that she respected this old convict more than she did his father. But was he being fair to her? After all, Delehanty was her countryman and Charlie Cole was not.

"A good day to ye too, Widow Quinn," came in a gruff voice from Delehanty, who nodded gravely to her, swept his gaze past the Coles, nodded to Prince Billy, and strode hurriedly away.

Jonathan saw how the woman looked after him. Yes, he had been right about her deep curtsey. It was a look of admiration she sent after the old Irishman. Suddenly she turned to Jonathan and said, "Mr. Delehanty asked me the other night of ye, Johnny. He takes an interest in ye."

"In *me*? Why?"

"Though he says ye be a bold fighter, he also thinks ye may be small size for yer age. I told him that ye were indeed smaller for yer age than most lads."

Jonathan bit his lip. The old lag thought he was a good fighter after having seen him fighting the butcher's boy, but he also clearly thought he was a runt. "Boyo" might mean "runt" to the Irish, and how tired he was of being called a runt.

To mask his disgust and save his dignity, Jonathan turned away from the two adults to say good-bye to Prince Billy. Even though Billy wouldn't understand what he was saying, he'd understand the grin Jonathan mustered up for him.

To his astonishment Prince Billy shifted the basket to his left arm, grabbed hold of Jonathan's hand with his right one, and pumped it in the proper manner while he said over and over, "Good-bye, farewell."

Molly told the Coles, laughing, "I taught him that yesterday."

Cole asked, "Will the blackfellows come back here later on?"

She looked at Prince Billy, shrugged, and sighed. Jonathan sensed that the ways of the aborigines were beyond her too, even if she could make herself understood to them.

A sudden gust of wind caught Jonathan full in the face, blowing yet another drift of dirty, powdery dust and dried animal dung into his eyes. This gust was particularly strong, and for a moment it blinded him. How the wind blew here! How often he rubbed his eyes lately! Now he had to wipe his entire face before he could see clearly again. When he could, he saw that Mrs. Quinn and Prince Billy had gone on. The woman's calico skirts blew in a bell shape about her waist, lifting up over her petticoats, while the blackfellow's rags whipped about like a ship's pennants.

Christmas came two weeks after the Coles went to the gold buyer's tent, and a pleasant evening was spent in the grog tent. That Christmas of 1851 was the strangest Jonathan Cole had ever known. In Massachusetts there had usually been snow on the ground, and he and his pa had spent the day dining at the home of some Cole relative. Last year in California they had left their claim and gone into town for a café dinner of steak and oysters packed in ice, but in blistering hot Ballarat they dined as usual on tough meat and damper. Though Jonathan's eyes were pink-rimmed and stinging, they went to Molly's tent anyway to make the day something special. With all his heart the boy wished he had a present for her. But he had none, for there was no money to buy one with, because they were so concerned about meeting the next month's license fee.

Molly had a gift for Jonathan. It was an orange, a fruit he had tasted only once before, at Christmas. It was a small one, full of seeds, but it smelled sweetly delicious as he carefully peeled it. Its perfume filled the air as he ate it, segment by segment, after offering to share it with Molly and his father. Although both refused, Molly did take the peel to flavor her next batch of the Knocker of Ballarat, and she thanked Jonathan kindly for the rind.

Turning to Charlie Cole, she warned, "If ye still be here come winter—this July—ye'd best buy Johnny a lemon now and then to keep off the scurvy sickness. It comes in mining camps as well as aboard ships."

"Thank you, but I hope to make our fortunes here before that time and have sailed for home."

"Aye, home?" Her face had grown suddenly somber.

"I'm sure sorry," said Jonathan, remembering that Molly and other transported convicts could never go home. He looked at the left-over orange rind, thinking what a strange, sad gift to anyone that was.

New Year's Day was a workday as usual. Shortly before the quitting gun sounded, Charlie Cole and a squinting Jonathan, whose eyes ached more and more each day, went to the gold buyer's tent again with another little bag of dust and nuggets. They were silent as they started back to their claim.

Finally Jonathan voiced what was bothering both of them. "Pa, do you think we'll have enough to pay the license fee this month?"

"I don't know for sure yet. It depends on whether we find some good-sized nuggets before then. Now don't you give up hope."

"I won't. I keep my mind on that nugget we saw in

Melbourne." As he spoke, Jonathan dug his rough-skinned knuckles into his eyes. At the moment they itched so that he could scarcely bear it.

His father caught him by the arm before he stumbled over a tent peg and fell. He said, "Johnny, let me see your eyes. You've been rubbing them all day long."

That was true. While they'd worked the rocker that day, he had paused often to wipe his eyes. The inflammation in them made tears run down his cheeks. The constant tearing caused the blowing dust to cake his cheeks with streaks of dirt and attracted flies by the dozens to his eyes. Half-blinded, he could scarcely see the screen he had to pour water through; again and again he wasted it, sloshing it down the sides of the machine.

Jonathan tilted his head to the afternoon sun and let his father look into his eyes. Charlie Cole said, "Your eyes are mighty red, redder than most people's around here by far. I don't know that it's just the dust that's doing this to you. Well, we'll wait till morning and see how they are then. It's been very dusty and windy today."

The next morning Jonathan's first words as he lay rubbing his eyes were, "Pa, is it near to daylight yet?" His father was awake; he had heard him coughing.

"Johnny, it's dawn! It's bright sunshine outside. Can't you see?"

"No, I can't get my eyes open," came the cry.

"Wait a minute. Let me come over and look at you." Jonathan felt his father's hand lifting his chin, then heard him say, "Your eyelids are puffed up badly. Do your eyes hurt?"

"Yes, and they sure itch too."

"Keep your hands off them. We'll take you to a doctor. There ought to be one in the camp. Maybe Mackay knows one."

"Pa, take me to Mrs. Quinn's tent. I bet she knows what to do about this. Doctors cost a lot of money."

"All right, Mrs. Quinn it'll be. I'll help you get there."

Molly Quinn touched Jonathan's face with gentle, cool fingers and then wiped away the tears running down his cheeks. She said, "I don't know what this is." Jonathan heard her turn to someone nearby and ask, "Do ye know what it'd be?"

Jonathan felt big hands trying to lift his eyelids; and when they parted in pain, he saw only a large blur in front of him. "'Tis the sandy blight," came the deep voice familiar to him. "I've seen it before, Widow Quinn. The flies and the dust, they bring it. I've seen men go blind from it."

"No, no!" came Charlie Cole's wail.

"Aye, sir, blind. Pray ye don't get it yerself, Mr. Yankee."

Jonathan reeled in terror. He felt his arm gripped by a powerful hand to steady him as he heard Molly ask, "Are ye certain 'tis the sandy blight, Mr. Delehanty? Can the boy be nursed?"

"I know this sickness. Nurse him and see if he can be helped."

Jonathan's arm was released, and then Molly's firm grip came onto his other arm. He heard her order his father, "Go for Surgeon MacBain, Mr. Cole. I'll put your son to bed here."

104

"Wait, Pa, wait!" Jonathan stood quiet for a moment, then said, "Mrs. Quinn, ma'am, I don't want you to catch this from me. I'd better go home with Pa and wait for the doctor to come to our tent."

Delehanty spoke now, not the woman. "If the Widow Quinn takes care, she won't get it." He added, "So, me boyo, in yer own time of sore trouble, ye can still think of a person other than yerself. 'Tis a thing to remember." He was silent, then he said, "Now, I'll be off to me own business. Good day to ye."

Molly ordered, "Come with me, Johnny. And ye, Mr. Cole, now go for the surgeon as I asked ye. Don't stand there doing nothing, man!"

From the sudden cool, Jonathan sensed that he had entered Mrs. Quinn's private tent. She led him inside a few steps farther, then took his right hand, guiding it until it touched cloth that felt like a ship's sails. As he touched it, it swung away from him.

" 'Tis a hammock. Can ye get up into it?"

"I think I can." Running both hands along the cloth, Jonathan pushed the hammock down and gingerly sat in it, then lay back, swaying in it.

She crooned, "That'd be right. Don't be frightened. The surgeon will come soon. Now I'll go out to me fire and bring the kettle to a boil and wash some cloths for your poor eyes. Call out if ye need me." She seemed to leave him now. He heard her muttering softly somewhere else in the tent, and then he heard the rustling of her long skirts as she left.

Jonathan sucked in his breath, fighting for control, and let it out slowly in what was almost a sob. He raised a hand to rub his stinging eyes; but before it could reach his face, it was caught by the wrist and held fast.

Terror waved over Jonathan in a flood. Who was attacking him when he was blind? His free hand shot up to grip the wrist of the hand that held his. "Mrs. Quinn, Mrs. Quinn!" he shouted, turning his head wildly to and fro.

# 7

# "A Credit
# to His
# Country"

Only a moment later Jonathan felt the stranger's fingers let go. He heard Molly say, " 'Tis only Prince Billy. I told him to keep yer hands from yer face."

Jonathan cried, "Prince Billy?"

"Aye, he and the others came back last night. The men have just now gone off with Mr. Delehanty, who wants them. Don't ye fret, Johnny, Prince Billy was over in the corner when I brought ye in here. The surgeon will come soon. Prince Billy will not come near ye again if ye promise to leave yer eyes be."

"All right, I promise." Jonathan lay back in the hammock. He was ashamed to tell her that he'd thought it was Delehanty or the other convict who'd caught his wrist to frighten him.

Before long Surgeon MacBain arrived with Charlie Cole. He lifted Jonathan's eyelids, grunted, and said, "The sandy blight if ever I saw it. I'll use the bluestone on the laddie now, Mrs. Quinn." And to Jonathan he said, "Laddie, this will pain ye, but ye must bear it while I scrape your eyelids." The boy felt himself pulled up by the shoulders to a sitting posture.

Charlie Cole cried, "Scrape his eyelids?"

"Aye, sir, I must! If it is not done, what's growin' under them will scratch his cornea, and he'll be blinded for life. Now, laddie, take a deep breath."

"Hold my hands," ordered Molly, grabbing hold of Jonathan's.

Though he'd been hurt in many fights, Jonathan had never known such pain as he experienced while the doctor lifted each of his eyelids and scraped them with a shiny crystal of copper set into a wooden handle. Though the boy gasped and crushed Molly's hands, he did not cry out.

"Good lad, good lad. Now lie down," ordered the surgeon after he finished. Jonathan let go of Molly's hands and fell back.

He heard his father's frenzied cry, "When can my boy see again?"

"Soon, but now he must not strain his eyes. He'd be best left here," said the Scottish doctor.

"Yes, yes," agreed Cole, "but can you cure him?"

"I think we may. Mrs. Quinn and I can perhaps do that. I'll come here tomorrow with the bluestone again."

Tomorrow? Be scraped again tomorrow? How long would that go on?

Charlie Cole asked his son's question.

"Who knows," replied the surgeon, "days for certain, perhaps weeks. Good day to ye, sir. I have other cases of the sandy blight to tend to here in Ballarat."

As he gathered his instruments, Surgeon MacBain instructed Molly. "Mrs. Quinn, keep the boy's eyes covered with cloth soaked in cold water. The cold will stop the pain and itching."

When MacBain had gone, Cole spoke to Jonathan, his voice strained and rushed, "Ah, son, I was proud of you just now! You're a brave boy, a credit to our country. You'll get well, I know it. I'll leave you now with Mrs. Quinn."

"Pa, what'll the doctor cost us?"

Cole spoke hastily, "Now don't you worry about that. You get well. Mrs. Quinn, will Johnny be all right in here? I mean, will he be all right with the native boy here too?"

"Aye, Mr. Cole. If I tell him to, Prince Billy will watch him for me."

"You're certain of that—that my son will come to no harm?" Charlie Cole sounded doubtful.

"He'll come to no harm at all. Now I'll go get wet, cool cloths to put on his eyes and take the pain away."

Cole said, "All right, then. Johnny, I'll leave you now too. I will go tell David Mackay what happened. I think I'll ask him to go partners with me while you're sick. We'll work both claims. Don't you fret. Our luck will run clear again soon. Mackay's a fine young man, a credit to our country too."

Jonathan sighed. His pa's idea was a good one. "Sure, Pa, talk to Mr. Mackay. You better go ask him right now."

Moments after his father had gone and Jonathan lay gritting his teeth against the pain, he became aware that someone was making noises not far away. It was Prince Billy singing, or rather crooning some very odd-sounding melody. It made Jonathan's mind go crazily to the old lag who had sung "The Wild Colonial Boy." Softly, to keep up his courage and take his mind off his eyes, Jonathan began to sing "Oh, Susanna." Now that he was alone it reminded him of home.

A week went by for Jonathan, a week of painful scrapings, then cold compresses, and of visits from his father. Charlie Cole had become partners with David Mackay, who said he felt obligated to help out because Jonathan couldn't work for a while.

Little by little the boy's lids parted, and to his great joy he could see, though still dimly. The daily scraping from Dr. MacBain was benefiting him, and by the end of the second week he was able to recognize by sight the hovering, red-haired woman; Prince Billy, his usually silent but constant companion; and anyone else who came to visit. By now he was bored of lying in the hammock, being spoon-fed, led by the hand to be washed, and of being treated like a baby or an invalid. But the Scottish surgeon refused to let him return to the Cole claim yet. One day he told Jonathan after the scraping, "Na, na, ye must bide here a bit longer, laddie. Diggin' in the dust is not what yer eyes need. When ye do go out, ye might think of wearin' a hat with a veil."

Jonathan's thoughts went to the mysterious Liam. He asked, "Is that why men wear veils in Australia?"

"It may be the reason."

Jonathan asked, "Do you know the big man who wears a veil and works with the one they call Delehanty?"

"Liam? Aye, I've seen him and know his name."

Molly, who was present at that moment, said, "Michael Delehanty asked of ye, Johnny, when last I saw him."

"What for?" asked Jonathan; but when Molly said she did not know, he returned to his previous question. "Dr. MacBain, does Liam come to you to have his eyelids scraped too? Have you had a look at his face?"

"Na, na, he does not come to me if it's the sandy blight that ails him."

"Oh," said the boy, disappointed. He told Molly irritatedly, "You can tell old Delehanty that I can still see things. Tell him too he won't have to look at me over the creek for a while yet."

"Tsk, tsk," reproved the Scottish surgeon. "That's not a good Christian attitude, laddie. I'll see you tomorrow."

That evening Jonathan had some good news from his father, who came visiting with David Mackay. How excited Charlie Cole was! While Mackay stood behind him smiling, Cole told Jonathan of the pocket of gold they had found on the Coles' claim. "It's four feet beneath the surface. We've got to dig down for it. We hope it isn't just a pocket that will peter out on us, but right now everything's going fine. We've found enough nuggets to pay both license fees for two months, as well as pay Dr. MacBain and Mrs. Quinn for nursing you and still have some left over. Digging's what we do from now on, no more panning, no more rockers."

"How big are the nuggets, Pa?"

"Pea-sized, but they're spread out on the ground, so you get them out with a pocket knife."

Mackay nodded, "You have to have good eyes to spot the nuggets."

Jonathan said sourly, "Well, I guess if you need good eyes that lets me out for a while, huh?"

Molly tried to comfort him. "Ah, Johnny, yer eyes are growing better every day now. It's soon ye'll be goin' back to yer claim, but now you'd better stay where you are."

"She's right," agreed Charlie Cole. "I talked to Dr. Mac-Bain. He says the dust's still bad even if autumn is on its way now."

Mackay put in softly, "Any boy would be bored here even if he had books, and poor Johnny can't use his eyes much yet. He needs something to do. Let me think. What can he do in here?" Jonathan watched the man look about him and all at once point to Prince Billy, who was standing against the tent wall. "Can he play checkers with this blackfellow?"

Molly said ruefully, "Prince Billy doesn't know how to do that." Suddenly she brightened and said, "There's something they could do—teach one another their language. Johnny could help me teach Billy English."

"Me? Teach anybody?"

"And why not, Johnny Cole? Exchange a word for a word with Billy. You two can begin the moment the men leave here." Molly's words were edged with her laughter.

While Jonathan lay amazed at the prospect of his becoming a teacher, David Mackay said, "And that, Mrs. Quinn, tells me it's time for us to go. We shall leave the boy in the fair hands of the beautiful queen of Ballarat and take our leave." He went out of the tent at once, leaving Molly staring after him.

Charlie Cole winked and said, "Good night, Johnny," and out he went after Mackay.

The lessons began at once. Molly beckoned Prince Billy over to Jonathan. She pointed to Billy's head and said, "*Boko*," then "head." Then she placed her hands alongside her cheek, closed her eyes, and said, "*Dura*, 'sleep.' Now, Johnny, ye teach the lad and he'll teach ye, I know. I have work to do."

After she had gone, Jonathan sat silent, trying to remember the word for "dog." Yes, he knew it. He said, "*Bokka*, 'dog.'" At that Prince Billy smiled and said, "Dog!" A moment later the native boy gave a few up-and-down springs, letting his hands dangle, and said, "*Jirra*." "Kangaroo," cried Jonathan. Prince Billy ran to get his spear and said, "*Naripal*." In turn the American boy pronounced the English word.

The following day Billy taught Jonathan the native word for "fire" by showing him Molly's campfire where supper cooked, "sun" by pointing to it, and at night the word for "star," which was *jewang*.

The lessons went on for another two weeks between very painful daily scrapings, soothing cold compresses, and periodic visits from a now-bearded Charlie Cole, who always entered dirty and weary from digging, but cheerful. He and Mackay were only waiting to get enough nuggets together to take to the gold buyer's tent before they made all Ballarat sit up and take notice of what they'd found.

One day when he came, Jonathan asked his father a question that was often on his mind. "Pa, what's going on with the two old lags over the creek? Do they act any different now that you've got Mr. Mackay as a partner instead of me? Has David Mackay's dog given their dog any trouble?

113

What's Delehanty up to? I can't ask Mrs. Quinn because she likes him."

Cole laughed. "Those Irishmen are so busy with the pick and shovel they don't give us a minute's notice. We don't pay them any heed either. It's digging pits with them now too. They've panned out their side of the creek. Sometimes I see those two blackfellows over at the Delehanty claim. As for Watchie, he's tied up on Mackay's claim when Mackay's digging on ours. His dog doesn't get loose to pester anybody."

"Pa, how's Joker?"

This made the man smile and say, "Well, our good friend Mrs. Quinn has done handsomely for us in everything else but in that dog she sold you. Joker's not worth much. He doesn't even go to the trouble of barking. I just keep Joker tied up for show. All he's got going for him is his large size."

Saying this, Charlie Cole nodded to Prince Billy, who came in and stood behind the hammock, pushing it so Jonathan swung slowly. Then he went out whistling.

A happy Jonathan told the native boy, "Pa's mighty pleased with himself." Craning his neck to look at Billy's expression, Jonathan said, "Billy, I guess you don't get what I mean. I wish I could tell you about Pa in English, but I don't know enough of your words for that. How can I translate 'good luck' and 'get rich'?" Suddenly the young American's face lit up. He pointed to where his father had just stood and then to himself and said a word he'd learned yesterday, *marandoo*, the aborigine word for "plenty." Molly said she had learned it from a native who had once pointed to a large number of lorikeets in the air and used that word with the native word for them.

Now Prince Billy said *"Bubba bubba"* the double word for "father." He knew how Charlie Cole was related to Jonathan, but he could not understand what Jonathan had said to him.

Jonathan looked at the blackfellow, wondering if either of the two adult aborigines was the boy's father. As he thought about them, he recalled what his father had just told him. So they had been seen across the creek at the old lags' claim. Was that where they were now? He hadn't seen hide nor hair of them all the time he'd been ill, though he knew that Mrs. Quinn sometimes fed them and Prince Billy in the mornings. Now he recalled that the men had gone off with Delehanty the first day he'd come to her with the sandy blight. What in the world would the two Irishmen want with the aborigines, even if they had by now learned to speak the native language well enough to be understood? Jonathan figured it must be something besides charity. Michael Delehanty didn't strike him as someone who would keep willing company with begging blackfellows.

How dull it was being kept inside, away from the winds, for so long. Jonathan found his thoughts running strangely, focusing at times on the people he had known at home in Massachusetts and on the people he had met here—Mrs. Quinn, Delehanty, Prince Billy, Dr. MacBain, and David Mackay. Out of the lot only the fellow Brother Jonathan, Mackay, seemed totally real to him, though every single day he saw the aborigine boy, the Irishwoman, and the Scottish doctor.

Jonathan dozed as much as possible in the swaying hammock. It was during one of those dozing periods, after Molly's cold cloths finally eased the pain of the latest scraping, that he became aware that Prince Billy had come out of his usual corner to stand near him. Jonathan removed the compress to see what Billy was up to. The young aborigine wasn't looking at him but at the closed tent flap as if he expected someone to enter. His eyes were wide and his mouth agape as if he were afraid.

"What is it, Billy?" asked Jonathan.

Billy shook his head and pointed to his ear as if to say "listen."

Jonathan listened. Yes, he could hear voices outside, a man's and a woman's. He rolled out of the hammock and went to the side of the tent, wondering if it was his pa or the doctor out there talking about his eyes. Whatever they were saying about him, he intended to hear, especially if they were trying to keep it from him.

No, he didn't recognize the man's voice, although he had heard it before. But where? It had an Irish accent. Delehanty? No. But it was someone he knew. Jonathan listened to it, straining his memory.

"Ah, Molly, me love, don't be tellin' me that ye be weary of my comin' to call on ye."

Jonathan heard Mrs. Quinn say softly, "Indeed I am weary. Do ye expect me to greet yer arrival with joy?"

"But, me love, I don't come so very often to see ye, do I, that ye can say I make a pest of meself? I niver come to partake of yer tea or yer fine cakes, do I?"

Suddenly Jonathan recognized the voice. It belonged to the big trooper who had broken up his fight with the butcher's boy. O'Connell, that was the man's name. He'd seen him now and then around Ballarat, standing guard duty beside the commissioner's tent.

Mrs. Quinn went on, "Na, na, ye never come to my tent with the diggers." She laughed gratingly and added, "Go about yer business. Make yer report to the commissioner. 'Tis yer assigned duty to do that. Go about yer business. We're done with each other now."

"Good day to ye, Widow Quinn."

Jonathan heard Molly say, her voice low and bitter, "Bad cess and bedamned to ye, O'Connell."

A moment later Jonathan heard her at the flap of the tent, untying it. Wondering mightily at what he had overheard, he hurried back to the hammock.

Just before she entered with a bowl of stew for his and Billy's meal, Jonathan glanced at Billy. Large beads of perspiration were running down his face, and he was shuddering. Why? Billy seemed to be afraid of the Irish trooper. Well, that was possible, all right. Something may have once happened between the two of them that he didn't know about. For whatever reason Billy was sure scared.

To Jonathan's surprise Mrs. Quinn was now smiling when a moment before she had sounded very angry.

Jonathan told her, "I thought I heard you talking to a man outside."

"A man?" She shook her head. "Na, ye must have been dreaming."

Jonathan said, "It sounded like the trooper who broke up the fight I had."

"Na, na, I saw the very same man ridin' off for Melbourne with the gold cart this mornin' early."

She lied. Jonathan wondered why but said nothing more to her. While he ate, he stole glances at Prince Billy, who had gone to sit down in the corner with his back to them, refusing to come near the food. Molly seemed not to notice Billy's behavior and soon went out again, leaving Jonathan alone to wonder at the things he had overheard and to try to fathom the actions of the woman and the native boy. There was some mystery here he did not begin to understand.

Six weeks went by for Jonathan, one day much like another. Each day he had an unpleasant visit from the surgeon and at least every other day a pleasant one from his father and David Mackay. They both seemed delighted when he and Prince Billy showed what each knew of the other's language.

"Fine and dandy!" Mackay cried. "You'll soon be talking like a native, Johnny."

Jonathan replied modestly and truthfully. "No, sir, it's mostly just words here and there. We aren't really talking yet, mostly pointing. I'm not sure his language has some of the words ours has."

"Well, if it does, you'll soon learn them," said Mackay smoothly. Jonathan's father nodded, smiling.

Jonathan could feel the seasons changing from hot summer to cool autumn even though he was not yet allowed to leave Molly's tent. At night he was glad of the blankets his father brought him. His sight improved daily, and he looked forward to going back to work the claim. MacBain thought he would be able to leave soon and that the fresh air at the creek bank would do him some good. However, he would still have to have his eyelids scraped daily.

Jonathan could always tell when it was Sunday, because

the sounds of pick axes hitting the earth stopped and Ballarat grew quieter. Molly's grog tent did a brisk business then, since the miners had free time. Because she was kept busy serving her customers, she was not in the smaller tent when Charlie Cole came one Sunday afternoon to see Jonathan.

The moment he entered Jonathan knew that something was very wrong. His father's color was bad, and he walked heavily with his eyes on his boots.

"Pa, what's wrong? Are you sick? Is Mr. Mackay sick?" asked Jonathan, his thoughts flying to Delehanty and the other convict. Had they beat up Mr. Mackay so he couldn't come visit him too? David had come the last six or seven times to laugh and joke with him about lying around in a hammock while the two men dug.

Cole lifted somber eyes to say, "No, but I'm afraid it's about Mackay, son." He sat down on a stool, not far from where Prince Billy sat, staring at him. Hands dangling between his knees, Cole went on tonelessly, "We haven't found so much gold lately as we did for a while. We found a pocket of gold on our claim, but that was all there was, just a pocket. Sometimes it happens that way. David was supposed to have taken the latest nuggets we'd collected to the gold buyer's tent yesterday afternoon." Cole looked up, blinking. "He didn't go there, Johnny. When he didn't come back to our claim, I went to hunt him up and learned then from the gold buyer that he had not come there at all. Then I talked to a man who'd seen him buy a horse and ride out of Ballarat. Watchie went with him, I guess. At least he was with Mackay when he left me yesterday. The dog never came back to me."

Jonathan cried, "Pa, what about the gold? Some of it was yours too."

"David took it with him. He took it all. He's a thief, and I boasted that he was a 'credit to our country.' " Charlie Cole buried his face in his hands. His voice was muffled as he said, "I went to the commissioner's tent and told him what had happened. He said he'd send out some troopers after David, but even if they caught him, it would be his word against mine that I owned some of the nuggets he had with him. Most of the gold he took came off our claim. Thank the Lord I paid the license fee and most of our debts just the other day."

Jonathan asked, "Have we got any money at all now?"

"Not much anymore."

Jonathan got out of the hammock. He said, "I've been here long enough. Tomorrow I'll start being your partner again. I'm going to go tell Mrs. Quinn that I'm leaving right this minute."

Cole didn't argue but said only, "All right, all right, Johnny." He stayed where he was on the stool as Jonathan went out.

The boy found Molly in the grog tent ladling out portions of the Knocker of Ballarat for two bewhiskered diggers. He came up to her and said quietly, "Ma'am, I'm going home with my father now. He needs me. Mr. Mackay's run off with our gold. Pa has to have a partner. Thank you for everything you did for me. I know he paid you some money for my keep, but I bet it's not enough."

Jonathan could not understand her expression, though he caught her deep sigh readily enough. She said, "Johnny,

Johnny, ye were a pleasure to me. I've got a fond spot for lads, ye know, and I reckon ye know why."

"Because of your boy, ma'am?"

"Aye. So go now with your father. He should not have trusted Mackay. I would not have. I didn't take to his ways —too charmin' and untrue he was. The 'queen of Ballarat' he kept callin' me. He did not mean it, and I knew he did not." She touched Jonathan's arm. "Do not put yer faith in charmin' folk, Johnny. Yer father should have seen into Mackay for a flatterer, but he did not."

"Neither did I, I guess."

Molly shook her head. "Yer father is forty years old and more. By now he should be able to take the measure of men. By now he should . . ." She bit her lip. "Ah, well, go with him. Keep yer hands from rubbin' yer eyes. Visit the surgeon as long as he tells ye to come. The sandy blight's not so bad now that the flies are fewer and the wind and dust's died down."

"Thank you again. Will you still keep Prince Billy with you?"

"I will. The men of his band have gone away again last week. He stayed behind here for yer sake, I think."

"For me, ma'am?"

"I think he did. He liked what ye taught him. Now go to yer father." She gestured toward the miners waiting for their cups of the Knocker in her hands.

There was little for Jonathan to take away with him, only a jacket and the blankets his father had brought him. He went over to Prince Billy, shook his hand, said the native word for "Good-bye," and went out into a bright cool day.

The Coles walked in silence through the camp, Charlie Cole staring at the ground and Jonathan looking around at the changes that had taken place in Ballarat while he'd been ill. The camp was larger now, crowded with more tents and diggers. Judging by its size, few people had left, and multitudes had come to swell the population. It was changing in other ways too. He saw a number of carts loaded with timbers, a sure sign that people intended to stay here and build a real town.

They passed David Mackay's claim, which was now only an empty square of earth. Cole explained, "David lived in our tent. I've got his tent stored." He laughed. "You can't say I haven't got something of his. I'll sell it tomorrow; I know where to get the best price. I know how to get things done in Ballarat by now."

The Cole claim was much as Jonathan had remembered it except that there now was a pit some four feet wide instead of a rocker. He walked to its edge, looked in, and saw that it went five or six feet down. Earth from it was heaped high about it on one side. A swift glance over the creek told him that their old lag neighbors had a similar pile of red dirt on their claim.

Looking around, Jonathan missed something. He asked, "Pa, where's Joker? Wasn't he tied up here when you left?"

Charlie Cole looked around too, then said slowly, "Joker was here when I went off to you. Maybe he slipped his knot again or chewed through the rope. He does that sometimes. Last week he disappeared, rope and all. David had a devil of a time finding him. He finally got hold of him over the creek. Mackay said that that dog over there was just about to take a big chunk out of him."

Anger swept over Jonathan, anger at Mackay and the two Irishmen and their fierce dog. He cried, "Pa, you didn't tell me that when you came to see me last week!"

Cole waved a weary hand. "I'd found a nice nugget that day and was thinking about it. It wasn't important. Joker didn't get hurt, and we got him back. It doesn't matter. Let Joker go."

Jonathan stopped for a moment, thinking about the dog. True, Joker wasn't worth much, but he was his dog and he had paid a shilling for him. It wasn't right that he should be wandering about Ballarat for anybody to claim. And it wasn't right either that the convicts' dog should attack Joker, who wasn't much of a fighter and meant no harm to anybody. It would be just like the dog to go over the creek again if he'd seen another dog, even if it had snarled at him.

"I plan to see where Joker is. I bet he's across the way again," said Jonathan as he sat down on the stump to take off his boots and stockings. The moment they were off he waded into the water.

Charlie Cole didn't try to stop him. He sat down on the stump himself and hunched over on it, clasping his hands.

Jonathan didn't look back at him as he swam across with silent strokes, being careful to keep the dirty water out of his eyes. If Joker was near the old lags' claim, he planned to get him and drag him back. No matter how much shouting and cursing and yelling he might get for trespassing, he was going to look for his dog.

The boy came up onto the opposite bank as quietly as he could. Under his breath he cursed Joker, who still had not learned to come at his master's whistle. The boy moved behind the shelter of the heaped-up earth and peeked around it. The dog was not to be seen, but the fawn-colored dog was, lying on his side sleeping in the sunshine.

While Jonathan looked around for any sign at all of Joker, Delehanty came shirtless out of the tent and bent over a basin set on a small table to wash his arms and chest. Looking at the man's broad back made Jonathan clap his hand over his mouth. The Irishman's entire back was a frightful mass of deep scars, crisscrossing one another. At one place in the middle, his spine showed through bone-white. Only one thing could make such scars, many floggings with a whip.

As Jonathan stepped backward, overcome with shock, the enormous man called Liam emerged from the tent with a skillet in his hand. This time he wore no veil. He looked directly at Jonathan, and a soft wordless growling sound came from his mouth.

One quick look left Jonathan gasping, fighting sudden nausea. He now knew why this man had always worn a veil. Liam had no nose! There was nothing in his pale face but two dark holes where his nose should have been.

Jonathan gave out a choking cry that made Delehanty turn around as the lags' dog leaped up, growling and snarling. Jonathan whirled around and ran. He flung himself into the creek and crossed it as swiftly as he could, fearing that the men or the dog would come after him. But there were no sounds but the dog's barking.

What had he done to make his and his pa's life even harder by spying on the Irishmen? He should never have gone over there. He should have forgotten Joker. Now he knew why strangers were not welcome over the creek and why Liam didn't go to Molly's tent.

To make Jonathan feel even worse as he came up onto the bank, he saw Joker trailing his chewed-through rope, coming along at an ambling trot from the direction of Mackay's old claim. He should have kept his head and his temper, realizing that the dog would have come back of his own account. Sociable Joker had probably just wanted to find some company when Pa had left him.

# 8

## The Winter Winds of July

Jonathan was so stunned at what he'd seen he didn't speak to his father of it at first. He only shook his head when Cole, after pointing to Joker, asked him if the swim had been worth it. Supper was a silent and dismal affair, with a damp Jonathan shivering beside the fire. His father was in no mood to talk, and neither was he. All he could picture in his mind was Liam's noseless face and the hideously mutilated back of Michael Delehanty.

Finally, as he and his father sat before their tent at dusk, he said quietly, "Pa, I saw the two old lags, and they saw me looking at them. I found out why the one wears a veil. He hasn't got a nose."

"No nose, Johnny?"

"That's right; and, Pa, the other one's back's so cut up that his backbone shows."

Cole said softly, "Oh, my God! I'd heard that convicts were flogged with leather whips tipped with iron."

"I guess that's what did it to his back, then; but why's the other one got no nose?"

"I can't imagine why. Good Lord, could there be leprosy here in Australia?"

Jonathan nodded; he'd heard of leprosy. He got up now and said, "Pa, I'm going to tell Mrs. Quinn what happened and ask her to tell Delehanty that I was only looking for our dog. Maybe that'll head off trouble for us from them."

"That's a fine idea, son. You told her that David Mackay ran off, I suppose."

"Yes," Jonathan hesitated, then added, "she didn't like him. She said he was too charming and told me not to trust such folks."

Charlie Cole sighed. "Yes, yes, she's quite right. I'm sorry about David, Johnny."

Before Jonathan left, he touched his father's shoulder and said, "It's all right. I can help you dig now. I see pretty good again, and I'll go to MacBain every morning till he tells me to stop coming. We'll be all right. We'll find some more nuggets. We've got a good claim here."

Cole put his hand over Jonathan's and patted it. "That's right. We'll find a nugget that's so big it'll set Ballarat on its ear."

Molly Quinn listened with a serious face to Jonathan's recital of his adventure on the old Irishmen's claim. Then she sighed and beckoned for him to follow her into the starry autumn night. "No nose ye say? Poor, poor man." She pulled her shawl closer about her shoulders.

"What's wrong with him, ma'am? Is it leprosy?"

"Na, not that; nor any accident. I believe it was bitten off for him. He's not the only noseless man who's been a convict in Van Diemen's Land."

"Bitten off? What kind of animal would do that to him?" As he spoke, Jonathan was aware that Prince Billy had come noiselessly out of the smaller tent to join them, as if he'd been summoned.

"No animal at all. It was a man, another convict. I've heard of it. 'Tis a thing convicts do to a man they think has informed on them—has told the guards that one of the lags intends to escape. I do not think Liam was guilty of doin' that or Michael Delehanty would have nothin' to do with him."

"I saw Delehanty's back. He's been whipped."

She said, "Aye, cruelly whipped—one hundred fifty lashes, or so the ballad about him says. I heard it sung the other night by a digger. Most men died under the lash but not Delehanty. Poor men, poor, poor men."

"I didn't mean to spy on them. When Delehanty comes here again, will you tell him I was only looking for my dog?"

"Aye, Johnny. I will. But ye've done them a hurt, ye know. It would please me if ye keep to yerself what ye've learned about them. Do that for my sake."

"Yes'm."

Drawing her shawl around her face, Molly went past

Jonathan into her smaller tent, followed by Prince Billy. Jonathan was left alone in the night to think. If Mrs. Quinn asked him not to talk about the old lags, he wouldn't. He owed her that favor for all she'd done for him. He knew Pa wouldn't say anything either.

As Jonathan walked back to the Coles' claim, his thoughts turned to his father, who had misplaced his trust in Mackay. It appeared that his father's judgment of people wasn't as good as it might be. There had been that other time in Massachusetts when he'd bought a cow from a friendly peddler and it had died a week later. From now on, he himself would have to see to it that they did not do anything else rash.

Jonathan's daily visits to Dr. MacBain for scrapings soon ended. For a time he went twice a week, then only once a week. Finally, to his great joy, he was slapped on the back and told not to return at all. The surgeon did warn Jonathan that summers would be dangerous for him because the sandy blight could strike him again. If by then he should still be in Ballarat and felt his eyes hurt and his lids swelling, he would have to begin the scrapings at once.

Except for his trips to buy meat and flour, he now spent the daylight hours digging, looking in the walls and on the bottom of their pit for seldom-seen glints of gold. Each time he came up out of the pit, he'd glance across the stream to see what was going on over there. He watched as, day after day, the pile of dirt on the Irishmen's property grew higher and higher, as if they were using everything they took out of their pit to make a high barrier. Jonathan guessed why—

to hide their claim from view. When he dug, Jonathan was just as careful to pile the dirt he brought up as a wall facing the creek also.

He and his father went occasionally to Molly's tent. She treated them as always, never once mentioning David Mackay or speaking of Jonathan's visit to the old lags' camp. Sometimes Prince Billy was with Molly and sometimes not. She said she never knew now when he might go off walkabout or when, if ever, he would return.

Jonathan was embarrassed because he was relieved not to see Prince Billy anymore. He felt he owed the native boy something for staying with him when he had the sandy blight. He wanted to give him a gift, but he had no money. Nor was there any spare tucker for him either. The Coles' finances were again becoming alarmingly low.

Neither Jonathan nor his father gave up hope, though. After all, other diggers kept finding large nuggets, so why not Charlie and Jonathan Cole. They could be worrying about coming up with the next month's license fee one moment, and the next they could be rich enough to take the road to Melbourne at once and seek a ship bound for California.

April passed and May arrived, with the weather growing colder and colder. Jonathan was glad that they were no longer working in the chilly creek water. By working from dawn to dusk in the mine, the Coles had amassed enough small nuggets to pay their monthly fee. They kept digging, praying that the next shovel of earth would be "pay dirt."

Early one morning while they were toiling, they had

an official visitor, Trooper O'Connell. He and another mounted trooper came riding upstream toward the Coles' claim. A shouting preceded them, passing along from digger to digger. "Hey, Joe! Hey, Joe!" The cry was a signal that troopers were about, patrolling and checking digging licenses. In this way, men who had no licenses or out-of-date ones could flee their claims or hide until these camp police had gone past.

Jonathan, who was aboveground cooking breakfast, called to his father down in the pit, "Pa, the troopers are coming to check the licenses. They're on our side of the creek this time."

"All right, Johnny, I'll come up right away."

By this time O'Connell had arrived at their claim. Towering over the Coles on a big white horse, he demanded, "Show me yer license paper."

Charlie Cole told him politely, "We just renewed it. I'm sure you'll find it in good order."

As Jonathan stood by watchfully, recalling the mysterious conversation he'd overheard outside Molly's tent, O'Connell growled at his father, "It'd better be in order, or things won't go well for ye, Mr. Yankee. Enough of yer blather, show me yer paper." As he gave the order, he took his glittering sword from the scabbard on his belt, whistled it through the air, and then held it close beside his shining black boots.

Charlie Cole looked warningly at his son, who needed no reminder to keep silent. Then he reached into the shirt pocket where he always kept the license and handed it up to the mounted soldier. While O'Connell examined it, he beat his naked blade against his boot menacingly.

At long last he said, "Aye, 'tis in order. Ye've got twenty days to go before it expires." And off he went, riding his horse slowly beside the other trooper's, with the cry "Hey, Joe!" resounding from all sides of the creek.

Once the riders passed out of earshot, Jonathan angrily commented to his father, "He wanted us to have an expired license. We disappointed him!"

"I hate to admit it, but I have to agree with you, Johnny."

The Coles stood on their claim and watched the Queen's troopers riding west. At each claim O'Connell seemed to repeat his actions, demand to see licenses, then take out his sword as a threat. At one claim a distance off, a digger dared to shake an angry fist at him. O'Connell struck the man about the head and shoulders with the flat of the blade, driving him down into the creek water, where he cowered in fear.

Watching that ugly scene, Charlie Cole wiped his dirt-stained forehead with his arm and said, "Now there's a man I don't want to meet up with again."

Jonathan told him, "Pa, that's the man who broke up my fight with the butcher's boy and called for Mrs. Quinn to look after me. I guess she knows him pretty well. He comes to talk to her sometimes. I heard them talking once outside the tent when I had the sandy blight."

"I'd say Mrs. Quinn has some strange friends. But he did you one favor, didn't he, although he doesn't seem to recognize you now."

Jonathan muttered, mostly to himself, "I'm glad he didn't. And I don't want to set eyes on that one trooper again!"

On a cold day in June Jonathan accompanied his father

to pay the license fee. He stood huddled in his jacket, listening as the Queen's commissioner talked to the older Cole. "Each time you come here, Cole, you ask me if I know anything more about your former partner. You'd best give up hope that he will ever be found. It's some time now since he left. He may have got to Melbourne, but I've had no word of him there. I think it far more likely that your countryman died somewhere in the bush trying to make his way over the mountains to the east. Or some bushranger took him on the road to Melbourne and . . ."

Charlie Cole interrupted bitterly, "And got our gold, huh?"

"Yes, and murdered your Mr. Mackay. Whatever, I am certain the nuggets he had with him will not be seen again by you." And always busy, the pink-cheeked commissioner beckoned to another digger who was standing in line to pay his license fee also.

By the time June ended, Jonathan was almost wishing for Christmas and hot weather, in spite of the fact that this would be the season for sandy blight. The winds of summer had been dusty and hot; those of winter were very cold. They didn't blow from the north as in America but came from the bottom of the world, Antarctica, and were chillingly cold. Even when he was ten feet down in the mine, Jonathan froze, because the soil was ice. He shivered as he used the pick and later pried for nuggets with a knife.

Except for the strictly enforced Sundays of leisure, one dull day was like another. First Charlie Cole worked alone in the mine and Jonathan hauled up dirt in a bucket, then Jonathan went down to relieve him. There wasn't room for the two to work together. Unlike panning, digging was lonesome work. After the sunset gun they ate supper, disappointed because they had found so little gold. The food was equally disappointing—always the same meat, coffee, damper, and dried fruit. There was no spare money to buy little extras, even a piece of horehound candy, Jonathan's favorite kind.

Finally, to Jonathan's sorrow, his father announced that they would have to forego visiting Mrs. Quinn's tent, because they could no longer spare the money for Spider and lemonade if they were to pay the next license fee. Jonathan regretted his father's decision and thought of going to Molly to tell her why they did not come. No, when their luck changed and Dame Fortune smiled, they'd go to her tent again and Jonathan would bring her a gift. A number of women, diggers' wives, had come to Ballarat by now. Shops in tents had sprung up to cater to them, selling fancy gewgaws like laces, crinolines, whalebone corsets, and fabrics. Outside one tent, hanging by its strings, was a handsome bonnet of black velvet with white plumes topping it. He would buy it for Mrs. Quinn, and she would be much admired when she wore it going about Ballarat shopping. She was truly the queen of Ballarat to him, much more of a queen than the real Queen Victoria in England.

July fourth was a day Jonathan and his pa had always commemorated in Massachusetts at a Cole family picnic. In Australia, of course, the American holiday wasn't celebrated. Here it was a work day like any other, one of toil in a chill rain that had started in the night and continued beyond dawn.

The Fourth turned out to be a day Jonathan Cole would

135

remember all his life! That morning he went down into the pit first. Because the previous night's rain had been heavy, there were at least three inches of water in the bottom of the mine. Jonathan scooped most of it out into a bucket his father lowered and hauled up again. Jonathan was about to fossick, to pry for nuggets, in the narrow hole's wet sides with his knife, when he heard his father shout from above.

"You come on up, Johnny, and bake us some damper before the rain gets worse and puts out our fire. I'll come down and use the pick for a while and see what I can do now that the rain's made the ground softer."

The pick? Jonathan had not planned to use the pick ax himself today, because the ground was already soft. Small rivulets of water wriggled down the sides of the pit and into seams in the dirt that had not been there yesterday.

Jonathan climbed up to the top and said, "Pa, do you think it's all right to use the pick now?"

Cole spoke brusquely, "Of course it is. Haven't I dug in the rain in California? Do you expect me to stop because of something so unimportant as rain? I dreamed about that nugget we saw in Melbourne again last night. There's one down there just as big! I know it!" Taking the pick ax with him, Charlie Cole went down the ladder into the mine.

Jonathan did as he'd been told. While he listened to the soft thudding of his father's pick, he mixed the dough for the damper and put it onto the usual flat stone to bake in the fire. Then he sat watching it, thinking how cold he was.

Suddenly he heard a sound, a rumbling of the ground beneath him, and felt a quivering. An earthquake? He'd gone through one in California and had been terrified. He got up to stare wild-eyed at the tent behind him. No, it wasn't an earthquake! The tent stood as it was before, wet and sagging.

"Johnny, Johnny!" came a soft, wailing cry. "Son!" it came again.

A rumbling, but not an earthquake. A landslide then? In two bounds Jonathan was at the brink of the mine, kneeling and looking down into it, shouting at the top of his lungs, "Pa, Pa!"

One of the damp walls of the pit had given way, and earth had fallen forward from it, pressing onto his father's body up to his chest. Jonathan knew that hundreds of pounds of dirt pressed on Charlie Cole, and it could shift and press even harder if his father tried to move. He had often heard miners talk of landslides and cave-ins, although he had never seen one before.

He cried, "I'll go get somebody to help you!"

He jumped to his feet and looked around him. A moment later he was on the claim of the three fair-haired men next to theirs, hauling at the coat sleeve of the oldest one, shouting, "Come, come!" and pointing.

To his great relief the man understood him, and he and the younger men came at a run. All three knelt to look into the mine together. Then the oldest man gave an order in his own language and one of the others ran to their claim and returned with two ropes. The smallest of them swiftly tied a rope around his waist and took up the second rope. As the other two men held the end of the tied rope, he went down the half-buried ladder into the pit. When he reached Charlie Cole, he pushed aside enough earth to tie the second rope under Cole's armpits. Then he climbed the ladder again. Once he was at the top, the oldest miner gave a sharp order and all three men began to pull on Charlie Cole's rope.

He came up slowly, gasping for breath, clutching at the rope around his chest until he was over the lip of the mine and lying on the muddy earth. His face was gray; blood ran down his chin in a thin red stream. Charlie Cole was hurt badly. Jonathan cried, "Don't you move, Pa! I'm goin' for Dr. MacBain right now," and leaving their claim at a dead run, he headed for the center of Ballarat and the surgeon's tent.

The small Scottish doctor helped Jonathan get his father into their tent. They laid him down and then removed the man's muddy clothing. Cole was coughing but no longer bleeding at the mouth. There were no bruises on his body that Jonathan could see, but he moaned when MacBain pressed on his chest. "His chest's been crushed, laddie. His lower ribs are broken," said the surgeon as he bandaged Cole's ribs tightly.

Jonathan cried, "What'll we do?"

"Keep him inside here. If he has fever or chills, come fetch me. Give him liquids. Ye may find him thirsty." MacBain shook his head. "Ye'd do best to send him to the Widow Quinn for nursing."

"No, no!" Charlie Cole sat up now, gasping. He coughed and fell back onto his blankets. "No, I already owe the lady thirty shillings I borrowed from her for the license fee I paid yesterday."

"Pa!" Jonathan had not known this. So this was why his

father didn't want to go to Molly's tent. He was humiliated that he had to borrowed money. "Pa, she'd take care of you anyway. I know she would."

"No, no, I cannot bother her anymore. I don't want charity. No one gives charity to Charlie Cole, no one!"

Jonathan spoke softly to the doctor. "We haven't got much money, sir."

"No matter, laddie. No matter. Pay me when ye can." MacBain patted Jonathan on the shoulder and went out into the rain.

Eight fearful days passed in the Cole tent. Charlie Cole had developed pneumonia. He coughed constantly and alternated between bouts of chills and high fever. Sometimes his mind was clear; at other times he spoke wildly, thinking he was home in Massachusetts talking to his sisters or to Jonathan's long-dead mother. And he was thirsty. Jonathan nursed him, pouring water, coffee, tea, and beef broth down his throat and begging him to eat. But his father had no appetite for anything but liquids.

As the days passed, the panic-stricken Jonathan watched his father grow more and more thin and pale. There was nothing he could do but bathe his body to keep his fever down and talk to him, imploring him to eat something.

On the ninth evening, after an endless day of fever and babblings, Charlie Cole fell into a quiet sleep. Jonathan was asleep also but near midnight was awakened by his father's voice asking, "Johnny, are you awake?"

"Yes, Pa." Jonathan sat up, jerking his blankets about him against the piercing cold. "Are you cold, Pa?"

139

"No, son."

"There was ice on a mud puddle yesterday morning."

Cole's voice sounded faraway. In a singsong manner he said, "You know, it's midsummer in Massachusetts now. The meadows are full of wild flowers."

"I reckon they are."

"Johnny, I never should have taken you away from there. We should never have gone to California. I've followed too many will-o'-the-wisps and made you go along with me. I've cheated you. You could have stayed with one of your aunts and gone to school."

"You haven't cheated me, Pa! Don't think that. I saw California and now I'm seeing Australia."

"Seeing Australia from the bottom of a hole?" Cole laughed softly. "I have cheated you. You should have gone to school these last years, not been doing a man's work. I wasn't as big as my dreams were. I wouldn't work our farm, and I wouldn't work for any other man for wages. No, I thought digging for gold would make me a rich and important man faster. And I was wrong. I never found enough gold. I never will. There would never have been enough for me if I had found it!"

"But we could find a nugget like we saw in Melbourne! That one came from here."

Cole's laughter was choked off by his coughing. "For you perhaps, Johnny. You might find such a nugget and be satisfied. But not me. I know myself now. I would have wanted another big nugget and another and another. I would have gone from one goldfield to another the rest of my life. And in time you would have grown tired of that life and left me. I don't think you and I are made of the same stuff; and for your sake, I'm glad you aren't."

"But, Pa, I wouldn't ever leave you." Jonathan crawled over to take his father's hand. It was very cold.

"Son, you would have had to leave. I know the doctor says I've got pneumonia. That's not my real disease, though. It's gold fever! You haven't got it yet."

"I do too have it, Pa. I got it in Melbourne when I saw that nugget."

"No, Johnny. If you'd really had the disease, you'd have been eager to leave the clipper ship bound for China to come here to Australia. You didn't want to leave it."

Jonathan sighed, "No, I didn't want to come here."

"Well, if you truly had a case of gold fever, you would have. You'd have pulled up stakes and ran to wherever you heard the accursed word 'gold'."

Cole paused for a long moment, then said, "I'm sorry, Johnny. Will you forgive your foolish old pa? Don't be like him, chasing rainbows for the pots of gold that might be there but probably won't be."

"Sure, Pa, but I haven't minded digging so much."

Charlie Cole let out a soft sigh. "Well, I've tried not to complain about my being so bunged up now, haven't I? At least I've done that for you, not complained to worry you even more?"

"You haven't complained at all."

"Johnny, have you done any digging since I got hurt?"

"No. I cleaned the caved-in dirt out of the mine. That's all."

"That's good that you did that. Fine. I feel like I could

sleep now. You'd best go back to sleep. I think I feel a little better." In the darkness Jonathan felt the pressure of his father's fingers, then felt him withdraw his hand.

As Jonathan rolled up in his blankets again, his father said, "You've been a mighty good son. No man could ask for a better one, or a better partner. Good night, Johnny. See you in the morning."

"Good night, Pa."

In saying that, Jonathan Cole said the last words he'd ever say to his father. When dawn came and the boy called to him, he didn't reply. Charlie Cole died sometime during the night, peacefully and quietly slipping away. When Jonathan went over to shake him gently by the shoulder, he did not move. His flesh was as chilled as the water in the creek, and his blue eyes were open, looking at the roof of the tent.

Jonathan said brokenly, "Oh, Pa, Pa!" He put his face in his hands, his eyes stinging.

Alone! He was alone in a foreign country, close to penniless, nearly friendless.

# 9

# The Queen's Trooper

Mrs. Quinn!

Jonathan staggered up and stood swaying, his eyes filled with tears. He'd go to Mrs. Quinn. He'd leave Joker where he was tied outside to watch over his father the short time he'd be away. Mrs. Quinn would help. She was a friend.

Sitting in her smaller tent, his head down, Jonathan spilled out the story of his father's accident and death.

The woman's eyes were somber and brimming with tears as she sat across from him at her small table. Finally she said, "I did not know. Poor man. Poor soul that he was. I was not told that he'd been hurt. I wondered that ye two did not come here at night anymore."

The boy told her brokenly, "Not coming was Pa's idea.

He didn't tell me that he borrowed money from you the other day. I guess he didn't want to come here and drink, because he'd be getting deeper in debt to you when he did." Jonathan waited a moment, then said, "I have to bury Pa."

"Aye, of course ye do. I'll see to that for ye, Johnny. There's a place here to bury folk. Others have gone there before him." Again she sighed. "Ye do not be Catholics, do ye?"

"No, ma'am. Pa and I are Congregationalists."

"Whatever that may be, I do not know; but there's a new chum minister here. I'll send someone to hunt him up and get others to make a grave. Now go back to yer father till someone comes to ye."

Jonathan got up. "Thank you, ma'am, for all you've done for me and my pa. I plan to work our claim myself till it's time for the next license fee to be paid. I think Pa would like me to do that. If I find gold there, I'll repay you what he borrowed. Maybe there'll be enough to pay the license fee too. I reckon I can keep the claim if I can pay."

"And what if ye do not find the yellow dodger, Johnny?"

He looked at the dirt floor of her tent and said, "That's a good name for gold, the 'yellow dodger.' She sure dodges me. Well, then I guess I'll have to start digging for somebody else and hope to save enough in wages to go back home."

"Home?" she asked very softly. "To California?"

"No, that's not home. I mean to Massachusetts, where I come from."

"How far is that?"

"I don't know how many miles, but I think it has to be

halfway around the world. Getting there would cost me a heap of money. Thank you, I'd best be getting back to Pa."

Her words were so quiet he scarcely heard them. "Ah, Johnny, ye were a credit to yer father."

"Pa said that too." With these words Jonathan fled the tent, running blindly toward the river through the downpour that had again begun. The rain beating on his face covered his hot tears.

Only four people attended Charlie Cole's funeral in a chill mist the next morning—Jonathan, the newly arrived minister, Mrs. Quinn, and the small Scottish doctor. The boy was a Congregationalist, the minister an Anglican, Mrs. Quinn a Catholic, and the doctor a Presbyterian; but the words from the Bible were familiar to all. Jonathan was glad that the young minister used the old prayers he knew. They comforted him.

While the minister read, Jonathan thought of his father and of his vain dreams of gold. He wouldn't go into business now, or see California again. He was being laid to rest in the alien earth of Australia. Perhaps he, Jonathan, would never go home either. He might end his days here too, going from goldfield to goldfield, or else working on a farm with sheep. Farming and mining—these were the two things he knew about, but he wasn't taken with either one. He could read, write, and figure sums well enough for his own purposes, but by no means well enough for anyone to hire him as a clerk. So he would have to work with his hands and his back.

After the funeral Molly Quinn walked back with him to the Cole claim. She looked at the soggy, dingy tent and the water-filled pit. Pulling her heavy shawl about her she said, "Ye need not stay here, Johnny. I'll take ye in."

"No, ma'am, I'll stay here long as I can. The claim is mine now since it was registered in both our names."

"Suit yerself, Johnny. But do not be too proud." The woman turned to look over the creek, then said, "Michael Delehanty's standin' there, before that mullocky heap." And she dropped a curtsey.

So the old lag was! He stood in the mist, his hat pulled low over his eyes, looking across at Molly and Jonathan.

The boy muttered bitterly, "Let him stare if it makes him happy. I don't care anymore."

Molly asked, "What did ye say?"

"Nothing. Nothing that matters."

Why tell her? She liked the old Irishman, who didn't even take off his hat to her.

Two weeks went by, weeks of loneliness, grieving, and hard work. August came in with cold weather and rainy skies. Jonathan worked alone in the pit, digging a little deeper but being careful with the pick as his father had not. He found some tiny nuggets, scarcely enough to buy food for him and Joker; but all the same that gold kept the two of them alive. He was determined to stay with the claim as long as he could hold it legally. The troopers could not come for him until the sunset gun had been fired on the last day.

By this time Jonathan truly did not expect Dame Fortune to smile on him. Perhaps she would be kinder if he worked for somebody else. Once he had to leave the claim, he intended to hire himself out to work for other miners. It was all he could do now. Digging alone wasn't a good idea anyway. It was too hard. A lone man ran up and down ladders all day long. He also had to cook and shop for himself, which took time away from digging. A man needed a partner when he mined.

Thursday, the day Jonathan would have to leave, came as a cool, clear day; and as he had expected, he lost title to the Coles' claim. He took down the tent and put it and his belongings into the one remaining wheelbarrow. Then he pulled up the stakes and threw them into the creek to float downstream. Without a glance behind him, he got hold of Joker's rope, took up the handles of his wheelbarrow, and left.

He pushed the barrow along the Yarrowee River and its creeks, asking the miners he passed if they wanted to hire "a strong boy who knew about digging from mining in California." All the men he spoke to were so busy digging that they only lifted their heads momentarily to look at him. They would either say "No" or "Sorry," then go back to work, turning their backs to him.

Just before sunset Jonathan came to the claim of two Americans. The young men had quit digging and were just fixing their supper as he pushed his barrow up to them. When he asked, "Please, can you use me to help you out here?" they looked at each other questioningly.

The taller one said, "I wish we could, kid, but you just ain't big enough yet to work for me. Mining's a man's work."

Jonathan answered quietly, where weeks before he would

147

have flared up in anger at the hint of being called a runt. "I dug with my pa for three years now."

As he started to turn away, the shorter man asked, "Do you want to sell that dog? We just came here the other day. Everybody else has got a dog but us. We could use one too."

Sell Joker? Jonathan looked down at the black dog. He was wagging his tail, looking hungrily at the meat frying in the skillet over the miners' campfire. Joker was thinner than when Jonathan had bought him from Molly months ago. He hadn't had much to eat lately either.

The boy's heart constricted. Well, why not sell the dog? Why should he have a hard time just because his master did? It wasn't Joker's fault that Pa had died. Too, he might as well get rid of him here, because any miners who hired him would probably already have a dog of their own.

"Will you feed him good, mister?" asked Jonathan of the shorter miner.

"Sure, I like dogs."

"All right. He cost me a shilling, so I'll sell him to you for that."

As he pocketed the coin, Jonathan handed Joker's rope to one of the Yankees. He said, "You'd better keep him tied up. He's inclined to wander off. Pa used to say he's mostly for show, not for biting." Then he patted Joker, who was intent on their supper, not on his old master, picked up the wheelbarrow handles, and left his countrymen. No, this Joker wasn't much like the one he'd had as a pet and ally in Massachusetts at all. He wouldn't miss him much, after awhile.

Jonathan knew where he was going—to Mrs. Quinn. If

anybody in Ballarat could tell him where to sell his belongings at the highest price, she could. Nobody digging seemed to want a boy his size. His best bet would be to get what money he could from the tent and tools and go back down to Melbourne. Maybe he could find work there on the docks. He would like being near the ships. He had not forgotten how much he'd enjoyed being aboard the wonderful Yankee clipper.

By the time he'd reached the grog tent, Prince Billy was waiting outside the other tent, as if he knew ahead of time that Jonathan would be coming. The native boy stared at the wheelbarrow, then came to it and touched the folded-up tent. He looked inquiringly into Jonathan's face and asked, "*Bokka?*"

Jonathan said, "I sold my dog. He wasn't much of one anyhow."

Jonathan left Prince Billy beside the barrow and entered the grog tent. Molly was stacking cups. She asked quietly, "Ye've given up the claim, have ye?"

Jonathan swallowed hard though he had expected this question and said, "Yes, ma'am, I've come to ask if you know where I can sell all my digging equipment. I don't need them anymore, and I can use the money. Then I'll go back to Melbourne."

"Will no digger here hire ye then?"

"No. I asked all day long."

"But ye did not come to ask me. Well, I shall hire ye. I have need of a lad to serve my trade and run my errands. The work won't pay ye much, however." She glared at Jonathan, almost as if she were angry, and said, "Don't tell

149

me ye scorn that kind of work. Work is work, even if it has to do with grog. Tomorrow ye can sell all. I'll tell ye where to go."

"Oh, ma'am!" Jonathan was nearly speechless. He added feebly, "I'm sorry but I sold the black dog I got from you."

Molly nodded, "So ye should have. There's no need of dogs when ye do not have a mine. I sold all I had, since there's no need of them in a grog shop. I won't take more of them. The small blackfellow guards me tents, and now ye can join him doin' that."

For the first time in weeks Jonathan smiled. Mrs. Quinn was indeed the queen of Ballarat. He told her, "Ma'am, take what you loaned to my pa out of what you pay me. I'll work for you if you'll do that."

"Aye, Johnny . . . " She would have gone on, but at that moment a man shouldered his way into the tent. It was Trooper O'Connell.

The soldier only glanced at Jonathan, showing no sign that he had ever seen him before. Then he jerked his head toward Molly and back again at Jonathan.

Molly didn't move. She ordered Jonathan, "Go to the other tent and make yerself a place to sleep before supper. I have business with the trooper here."

Quick to obey her, Jonathan left but hesitated before he went to the wheelbarrow to get out his blankets for the night. Mrs. Quinn had frozen when O'Connell had entered her tent. No, she didn't want the man there. Remembering what he'd overheard before, Jonathan came close to the tent. He could hear Molly speaking from inside now, and again her voice sounded angry. This time the deep replying voice of the trooper was angry too, but now they weren't speaking in English. Jonathan guessed they were conversing in Gaelic, the tongue she had once told him the Irish spoke among themselves.

The talk went on briefly, and then O'Connell burst suddenly out of the tent, grinning broadly. He was intent on putting something into his blue coat and did not notice Jonathan. The boy quickly moved away from the side of the tent and returned to his barrow. He saw that Prince Billy stood beside it, staring after the trooper. He was perspiring as he had done the time before. His eyes were fixed on the man's broad back, and under his breath he muttered some sort of chant. Yes, Billy was definitely afraid of O'Connell. But why?

That evening Jonathan tried to speak with Mrs. Quinn about the soldier's visit. He did not mention the two conversations he had overheard but only asked, "Ma'am, did you know Trooper O'Connell in Ireland?"

Molly didn't look at Jonathan as she snapped out, "I did! He hails from County Meath in Ireland and is the son of my dead husband's aunt. He made me acquaintance in Melbourne when he came to Australia with other English soldiers. And now he's been sent to Ballarat to do the commissioner's bidding. But, enough of this talk of him. Me stew pot needs a good scourin' out, or we'll all be poisoned by it come suppertime some day soon. Be off with ye!" And she lifted her apron and flapped it at him.

Jonathan did not move. He persisted with his questions. "Do you know why Prince Billy is scared of the trooper? He sure is."

Molly shook her red head. "I have no idea. Why do you think Billy is afraid of O'Connell?"

"I saw his face when he came today. If you'd seen it, you'd know he's afraid too."

She shrugged. "Perhaps Billy fears all the troopers hereabouts. That would be wisdom on his part, indeed." She frowned, then shivered in spite of the warmth of the tent. "Ah, perhaps the lad can see what's hid from the likes of you and me. They say that the blackfellows sometimes can know ahead of time the way things will turn out. Now, Johnny, get to that cook pot and leave off yer blathering."

Jonathan found working for Mrs. Quinn to be mostly pleasant. He liked running errands for her in Ballarat, going off with Prince Billy in tow, both of them carrying baskets. He didn't mind washing out cups and bowls, stirring laundry in the big cauldron over the constant fire, and baking damper for the three of them. Nor did he mind scrubbing her tables and helping mix the Knocker of Ballarat.

But he did not like serving the diggers who came to the grog tent. He lacked Molly's easy, joking way with the men. He worried that he might do something to anger her or one of them. When they came inside demanding something to drink, he was nervous that he might spill liquor on them, or stumble over their feet, or give them the wrong change when they gave him English coins.

He saw immediately that the various men drank differently. Some came in swaggering; they would call for a cup of rum, drink it down at once, and call for more. Others, hollow-eyed with fatigue, would ask for a large cup of grog and then spend the night hunched over it, looking off into the distance, not speaking. Occasionally, some grew very drunk and had to be coaxed outside by Molly or even dragged out by her and Jonathan. Sometimes she would set them in a corner and let them nod away to peaceful sleep.

A number of diggers could not speak English and would point to their mouths, then to the barrels of rum and gin. Molly herself served these men. Jonathan marveled at her way with them, wondering how she could understand what they wanted; somehow she did and always left them happy with something in a cup in front of them.

Jonathan never saw any barneys, or fist fights, while he was working. There were seldom even loud words said. Men who were becoming noisy were told to be quiet by others. It was as if the diggers were protective of the Widow Quinn and valued her friendship.

Miners of every age, disposition, and nationality came to Molly's place, drank, and left. Several times Jonathan served Michael Delehanty, giving him a cup of rum as requested. To the boy's relief, the old lag never said anything to him, though Jonathan was always uncomfortably aware that the man's eyes followed him as he moved about the tent serving other diggers.

Once after they had closed for the night, he commented to Molly on Delehanty's stare. She said wearily, "I had not noticed that, Johnny. Do not be afraid of the men who come in here. They are all friends to me."

"Yes'm." Jonathan's thoughts went to one he suspected was not, the big Irish trooper, O'Connell. He was tempted to mention him by name but thought better of it and held his tongue. That man was Molly's business, not his.

Jonathan had been with Molly Quinn for four weeks
when Trooper O'Connell came again to the grog tent. Jonathan was once more ordered outside and once more he
stayed by the tent flap to listen. This time he was afraid. He
heard the man start to speak the same foreign language, but
this time Mrs. Quinn would have none of it.

Jonathan heard her cry, "I'll speak no more Gaelic to ye,
a man of Ireland who'll put on the Queen's blue coat and
take her pay and serve the English government that has
treated Ireland so cruel. 'Tis the last month I'll give ye any
money, O'Connell. I've almost got the money saved to pay
me license fee, so I'll soon be sellin' grog with the commissioner's kind permission. This will be a licensed tavern, no
more a sly grog shop that ye troopers can come burn down
if the commissioner finds I have no license. I'll build a fine
house of timber and call me public house 'The Harp.'

"It was yer duty to check the shops of Ballarat for sly
grog. Ever since I came here I've paid ye every month to
protect me and tell the commissioner that I sold naught but
tea and coffee and cakes. Each month ye've demanded more
shillings of me, when our first agreement was for eighteen
only. Ye kept me secret for yer own profit, not for any favor
to me.

"If I had not had to pay ye so much each month, I would
have been able to buy me license long ago. Ye don't want
me to have it! It suits yer purpose for me to sell sly grog
forever. But no more. I'll soon be rid of ye, Trooper O'Connell. If ye try to inform on me to the commissioner now, I'll

tell him that ye have protected me all this time. He can burn me out. Then I will pay for a license and start over again to sell grog legally." Molly's voice was low, controlled, and hissing. "This time I must give ye forty-five shillings. 'Tis more than a digger pays each month for his license fee. Ye do not be a soldier but a bushranger."

Jonathan heard the man's deep laughter, then came his words, "Ah, how ye do go on, Molly, me love. I'll see ye next month on this same day, and I'll be askin' fifty shillings from ye then. Good day to ye, Widow Quinn."

Hearing his final words, Jonathan hastened around the corner of the tent. There he stood for a time chewing on a ragged fingernail, deep in thought. He recalled what Molly had said to him at their first meeting that, although her trade was not a legal one, she had no fears. This was surely what she had meant. Her customers would not tell she sold liquor illegally, because they liked her and the grog she sold them. This big trooper had not told, because he wanted her to go on paying him forever. No wonder she was angry. No wonder she hated him!

But what could he, Jonathan Cole, do to help? He could not go to the commissioner. Nor could he threaten big O'Connell. The trooper would only laugh at the undersized boy. Jonathan sighed, regretting his helplessness. He loved Mrs. Quinn; and though she had not said so in words, he knew she loved him too. Sometimes she had absentmindedly called him Pharic, her dead son's name. She treated him with gentleness, smiling and laughing; but sometimes she was stern, making Jonathan suspect this was how real mothers behaved.

Though Prince Billy's ways remained alien to Jonathan, Trooper O'Connell's did not. He was only a villain. After much thought, Jonathan made up his mind what to do. He would keep secret from Mrs. Quinn what he had overheard but would refuse to accept any wages until she had enough money to buy her license. After all, it was partly his and his father's fault that she did not have her license money yet, for she had loaned the older Cole thirty shillings when he needed to pay his own fee. Jonathan could not keep Trooper O'Connell away from her. But at least he would help Molly free herself from him sooner.

How nervous Molly seemed the day he was to come! Jonathan watched her closely that evening, seeing her glance again and again at the open tent flap. Where she generally had some courteous, welcoming words for old Michael Delehanty, now she only bade him a curt "Good evening." Her face was somber, her jaw set, and her eyes angry.

Delehanty noticed this too. For the first time the old lag spoke more than the single word "Rum" to Jonathan. He asked, "What ails the Widow Quinn, boyo?"

"How should I know that?" replied Jonathan, who was carrying two cups of gin to miners at another table.

Delehanty was the last to leave that night. He took a bottle of rum with him. Jonathan knew by now that he bought this for his partner, Liam. Relieved to see him go, Jonathan watched him stride off with the moonlight on his shoulders. As the old lag passed Molly's smaller tent, the two aborigine men who had been sitting nearby arose and followed after him. The Irishman turned to look at them, nodded, and then walked on with them following behind. What business did they have with each other?

Shaking his head, mystified as always by Delehanty and the natives, Jonathan watched Prince Billy leave Molly's tent and pass him, going into the grog tent. He wished he could question Billy about the two men and the old lag, but he couldn't make himself understood. Besides it wasn't Delehanty or the aborigines who concerned him tonight but Trooper O'Connell. Jonathan knew he would come, and probably soon. Mrs. Quinn was already closing up for the evening.

As Jonathan went back into the grog tent, she told him, "Johnny, wipe the tables and then go to the other tent. Take Billy with ye."

"Yes'm!" Well, he would clean up, but he would not go away. Not right now anyhow. When her back was turned, Jonathan ducked under the largest table and sat down to wait, his legs drawn up to his chest. In his hand he held a bung starter, a small clublike wooden instrument used to open a barrel of rum. He didn't know what he would do with the thing but having it would make him feel braver when O'Connell showed up. He was afraid—for Molly and for himself—but tonight he wasn't about to leave her alone with the trooper. Prince Billy came scuttling over to him on his hands and knees and sat down beside him. He did it so swiftly and silently that Mrs. Quinn had not noticed his action anymore than she had noticed Jonathan's.

Jonathan had no idea how long they waited under the table. It seemed to him a long time before he heard the

157

clopping of a horse's hooves coming toward the tent. Then he heard a man grunt as he dismounted, and an instant later Trooper O'Connell was at the entrance of the grog tent, filling it with his bulk. He stood, hands on his hips, to say, "Well, me darlin', I've come for me fifty shillings."

Jonathan saw Molly, who had been sitting at the other table, arise wearily. She said, "Which ye'll not be getting. Ye'll leave me tent at once. Tomorrow I'll buy me license. The money I got tonight will give me what I need."

"Will ye now?" Saying that, O'Connell came inside. "Will ye want me to call the commissioner out of his bed now? He will ask ye for yer license, since he can see with his own eyes what ye've been up to here."

"No, I'll pay him tomorrow." Molly spoke through gritted teeth. "I'll not pay ye now, O'Connell. I'll never pay ye agin. Leave me!"

"Ye convict slut, no convict says No to me!"

Jonathan saw the trooper walk over to Molly. She stood unmoving, her head thrown back and defiant. As he came up to her, she hit at him in an open-handed slap. The man laughed, grabbed her wrist before the slap struck him, and, still laughing, cuffed her head. He gave her a push that sent her reeling away from the table toward a smaller one that held her store of liquors. Tottering backward, she lost her balance and fell, her head striking against the edge of the table. Then she crumpled to the dirt floor.

"*Yah!*" yelled Jonathan Cole, rolling over and bringing the bung starter down on one of O'Connell's booted feet. The man bent down and jerked the boy up by the collar. He cried out in anger, "Wot's this here?"

158

Holding Jonathan firmly, the trooper went over to peer at Molly Quinn. He touched her with the tip of his boot and growled, "Woman, I want fifty shillings from ye. Get to yer feet and give me what I came for. I ride for Mount Alexander tonight and have no time to tarry. Get up, I say."

When he received no response, he went down on one knee and stared at Molly. With the hand that didn't hold Jonathan captive, he lifted her head slightly. When he brought his hand out from under her, it was smeared with bright blood.

He whispered, "Dead? The bedamned woman's dead! I didn't have it in mind to kill her."

Rising, he clapped a hand over Jonathan's mouth and, carrying him, went softly and quietly out of the tent.

As he left, Prince Billy crawled out from under the table, went over to Molly's body, and, rising up to his knees, began slowly to rock to and fro, crooning tonelessly.

# 10

## Feather Shoes

Ballarat slept the sleep of weary men trying through the night to gather the strength for another day of frantic digging. No one but Prince Billy had seen the soldier leave the grog tent with Jonathan. No one heard O'Connell hiss into Jonathan's ear, "Hold yer clack or I'll break yer neck for ye. I'll be puttin' ye up on my horse in front of me now. Give me no trouble and it'll go best with ye!"

Numb with shock, Jonathan nodded. He knew that "hold your clack" meant to keep quiet, and he did keep silent as the trooper lifted him and plopped him down in front of the saddle and then mounted behind him.

The moment the man mounted, he put one large hand over Jonathan's mouth and with the other managed the horse's reins. Jonathan didn't think of struggling now but only of Molly Quinn, who lay dead on the floor of her tent. Generous, good Molly. He couldn't weep for her. He'd grieved so recently for his father that now he felt nothing but a sharp aching in his throat, which came of knowing that once more he'd lost a loved one. Molly Quinn too was gone.

A sudden anger passed like a spear through his benumbed brain. First his pa and now Molly Quinn, both had died for money's sake—Pa for the big nuggets of gold and Mrs. Quinn because she refused to pay O'Connell his fifty shillings.

O'Connell! With a start Jonathan realized what was happening to him. Molly's murderer was riding in back of him, pressing Jonathan's back against his blue coat. The trooper's horse was trotting now, threading its way around the tents. O'Connell was heading toward the Yarrowee River. A few minutes later the horse went down into the sluggish stream and began to swim. Cold, dark waters enveloped Jonathan up to his waist. As they emerged on the other side, tethered dogs barked briefly at their passage. It was very late now, and no one came out of a tent to see who was riding by.

Once past the last of the tents, the trooper guided his horse onto a narrow track that ran between ranks of tall gum trees. The road soon forked, and the man chose the right-hand path. Now he spurred the horse into a canter and took his hand away from Jonathan's face.

"Now yell out all ye want to, boyo! No man'll hear ye."

Jonathan Cole twisted around to look up into his face, shadowed by his visored cap, and cried, "Where are you taking me? Let me down."

The man said mockingly, "Far, far away, me lad! Far enough away that ye'll never be a bother to me again and tell anyone the manner of Mrs. Quinn's dyin'."

Jonathan sucked in his breath in terror. He now realized he was being taken into the bush, the wilderness beyond Ballarat, to be murdered too. No one would know. Afterward the soldier would ride back to the camp as if he'd come from Mount Alexander, the other gold camp. No one would suspect him of Molly's death. Even though Prince Billy had witnessed the murder, no one would believe him. Billy probably would not go to the commissioner's tent at all.

Jonathan mumbled, "You didn't mean to kill Mrs. Quinn. Don't kill me too."

The soldier said, "No, I did not have that in mind. I was only after teaching the woman a lesson. And I don't have it in mind to kill ye either." As Jonathan slumped with relief, the man went on, "Na, when I've gone far enough, I'll set ye down in the bush. Ye'll niver find yer way back to camp. I don't mean to hang for killin' anyone."

Leave him alone in the wilderness! It would be as certain as killing him outright. It would be a slower death, but death from starvation all the same. Sick with misery Jonathan kept silent. He'd taken O'Connell's measurement. He was not a man who would listen to a plea for mercy.

They rode through rolling country until the moon was down. Then they halted at a stream in a dark meadow ringed by black trees. Still sitting his horse with Jonathan in front of him, O'Connell let it rest a time and drink from a pond. A half hour later they were on their way once more, moving at a walk through a forest of red-bark gums.

White cockatoos, galahs, and lorikeets flew from tree to tree ahead of them as they traveled, always northward. Once the horse shied as it came upon a group of kangaroos feeding at dawn. The creatures rose up to stare, and all but a huge gray male bounded off. The six-foot-tall kangaroo stood still, waiting for O'Connell to get the horse under control again, then jumped slowly away to join the others.

The trooper said, "That's a forester kangaroo. It might attack a dog or even a man on foot. That one may niver have seen a horse till now."

Jonathan said nothing, only looked about him, trying to fix certain trees in his mind. But there were so many of them, and they were so much alike. Halfway through the morning O'Connell once again halted. He reined in his horse at the bottom of a small hill, where there were fewer trees than usual and some undergrowth. Taking Jonathan under the arms, he dropped him down over the side of the horse.

"This is where I'll leave ye. I've been here before and know me way to Mount Alexander." He shook his head. "'Tis sorry I am that ye saw me strike the Widow Quinn. If ye had not been there to see that, ye would not be here at this moment; and ye would live to become a man."

Jonathan was not surprised by this farewell speech. He had expected that the man would excuse himself with words, and he was prepared for it. He refused to cry in front of him. Instead, he turned his back on the trooper until he heard the *clip-clop* sound of the horse leaving.

Then he sat down on a nearby log. For a long time he stayed there with his head in his hands, thinking about what he should do now. He would try to make his way to civilization, but what direction should he take? A sound from inside the hollow log made him go over to its end. He hoped there was an opossum inside, for Molly said it could be eaten. A moment later a slender brown snake emerged and slithered past him. Jonathan jumped back, startling it. It turned its head and hissed at him. The boy shivered and let it alone.

He climbed now to the top of the hill to look about him for landmarks he might recognize, but he saw nothing but trees. At the bottom of the hill, he sighted five yellow dogs nosing along the ground as if on the scent of something. As he gazed at them, one looked up. They were dingoes. He had heard them yapping in the distance during the night. Had they scented and followed the trooper's horse? That could be why they were here.

Jonathan looked feverishly about him and found a gum tree with a branch he could reach. He grabbed it and pulled himself up into the tree. The dingoes came up the hill, sniffed at the bottom of his tree, and sat down looking up at him. They stayed there until sunset, then trotted off. All this time, Jonathan never took his eyes from them.

Exhausted by his vigil, the boy fell asleep in the tree. He awoke near sunrise. He needed water badly by now so had to come down. After looking about him carefully to make certain the dingoes were gone, the boy climbed down from the tree and walked over to some jutting rocks nearby. He had seen the dingoes go over to them to drink. He now filled his hands with rainwater caught in a depression and drank gratefully.

He wandered a bit that day looking for food but found

nothing to eat. That night he returned to the hill and slept in another tree. He was awakened just after dawn by noises below. The dingoes again? Looking down, he saw two gigantic brown-feathered birds. They were walking about, their heads bent low, pecking at insects in the soil. Jonathan estimated that the creatures were as tall as he was. They were emus, fearsome-looking birds with huge, sharp-clawed feet. The boy felt sure they would not be shooed away like barnyard chickens. He would have to wait where he was until they themselves decided to leave.

Jonathan waited a long time, afraid to shift his posture and call attention to himself. Finally when he was about to risk moving a cramped leg, the emus suddenly raised their heads and looked to one side of the clearing. An instant later a spear sped through the air and buried itself in the body of the emu farthest from Jonathan's tree. As the great bird sank down, its companion squawked and, in a flurry of feathers, ran off.

Holding his breath, Jonathan Cole waited, terrified. He soon saw two tall aborigine men come out from behind some trees to his left. They were naked, their faces and bodies painted with white symbols. They were the wildest blackfellows he had yet seen. Jonathan felt like whimpering but stayed quiet and motionless, watching as the men went up to the fallen emu to pull out the spear.

Then to his horror they came toward him and halted at the base of his gum tree. For a long, dreadful moment they looked directly up at him. Then the taller man raised his spear, called out a word, and a young native came wriggling out of the nearby undergrowth. He came toward the men and held out a bag of blue cloth to the one who had summoned him. The boy walked with a limp, dragging one foot.

Jonathan shouted in joy, *"Billy!"*

Prince Billy looked up at him and grinned. He then made a gesture and called out "Come" in English. Jonathan at once shinnied down the tree. Now he recognized the painted men as the two blackfellows he'd often seen in Ballarat with Prince Billy.

He guessed at what had happened. After Prince Billy had seen Molly killed, he had gone to get the men. The three natives had tracked O'Connell's horse through the bush. Jonathan was not surprised that they could find him, for Molly had once spoken of the great, almost magical skill the aborigines had as trackers.

The adult blackfellow who held the blue bag reached inside and pulled out a piece of stonelike damper. He gave this to Jonathan to gnaw on, and then offered some bad-tasting water from a leather bag slung over his shoulder. As the famished Jonathan ate, he suddenly recognized the blue bag as belonging to Mrs. Quinn. It had contained trinkets and sewing supplies. Why had Prince Billy brought it here?

The adult natives now did something Jonathan found odd. He had expected them to cook the emu they speared. Instead, they went over to it and started plucking the largest feathers from it. Taking Molly's sturdiest sewing needles and some strong black thread, they sat down and began to sew the feathers together. Astonished, Jonathan watched the swift, deft stitchery as each man made two identical objects from the leathery feathers. As they stitched they chanted the same low tune, ending together as they put down the nee-

167

dles. A moment later, the two natives put the oval-shaped brown objects on their feet, stood up in them, then bent to grab their spears.

"*Kurdaitcha!*" exclaimed Prince Billy, pointing to the shoes.

Jonathan stared at the men. He felt he was in the middle of a dream as he watched them go off to the left at a lope, now and then bending low to look at the ground. Were they going hunting again?

Suddenly Jonathan thought he knew. They were tracking the Irish trooper and his horse. The boy gagged on the dry food, remembering the carbine on O'Connell's saddle. Jonathan glanced at Prince Billy, who was looking most unconcerned. All at once Billy pointed to the slain emu, said the aborigine word for "fire," and handed Jonathan the blue bag. When he opened it, Jonathan found flint and a tinder box inside. He nodded, understanding. While Prince Billy plucked and cut the emu, he was to make a fire. They would cook the bird and dine on roasted meat. Well, that would suit him just fine.

After they finished eating, the two boys packed the remaining roasted meat in Molly's bag and left. Prince Billy led the way. Jonathan had no idea where they were going, but he trusted the young native.

For two days the boys walked through the forest. Now and then they saw kangaroos, wallabies, and more dingoes, but they were not bothered by them. Once they spotted a huge, five-foot-long blue goanna and carefully walked around it. Although the lizard was not venomous, it was safer not to disturb it. Another time Prince Billy touched his arm and pointed to the tangled mass of floating poisonous snakes in the slow, flood-swollen waters from which he was about to drink.

Halfway through their third day of walking, Prince Billy stopped and listened. Jonathan could hear nothing but the usual grating calls of currawongs and the screeching of hundreds of cockatoos in the trees around them. Suddenly Billy threw himself to the ground and put his ear to it. In a moment he was up again and said, "Horse." The two boys ran to a nearby grove of gums and hid themselves.

Was it a bushranger? Jonathan gripped the tree branch he carried as a club and crouched low behind a tree with Prince Billy, waiting. Soon a bay horse came walking toward them from the west. Jonathan saw that it was saddled and bridled but riderless. It was led by a naked blackfellow, followed by another. Both wore shoes of fraying feathers.

Jonathan recognized the horse; it was Trooper O'Connell's mount. Both boys came out of hiding. The aborigine leading the horse gave Prince Billy the reins. He said something to the boy in their own language and then, without another word, both men disappeared into the trees behind Jonathan.

Where was O'Connell? How had the blackfellows come by his horse? As Jonathan walked around the animal, his question was answered. The blue saddlecloth was tinted a dark brown in one place. Jonathan touched the spot and found it stiff. Blood! He shuddered. Trooper O'Connell hadn't been hanged as he deserved, but all the same he'd had justice done to him for Molly's sake. He had probably been no more aware of the aborigines stalking him than the emu or he himself had. How swiftly and accurately the spear had been thrown at the great bird. The soldier's carbine was still in its saddle scabbard. It would have been of no use to him if he could not even see his avenging hunters.

"Come," ordered Prince Billy, and he led the bay as the two boys started off again.

Some hours later Jonathan Cole heard a loud booming. It was the sunset gun of Ballarat. Prince Billy had brought him home.

It was fully dark by the time Jonathan and Billy entered the commissioner's tent. With Prince Billy beside him, Jonathan spoke with the Queen's representative. The gray-whiskered man listened carefully, frowning all the while. Then he said, "You say the horse was delivered to you by two natives and that O'Connell has probably been killed by them? Well, I do know he never arrived at Mount Alexander. He was to bring a prisoner back here to me. And you say you saw these two blackfellows sewing shoes from the feathers of the emu they had speared?"

"Yes, sir, I did." Jonathan now gave him Molly's blue bag, adding, "They used needles and thread from this. It belonged to Mrs. Quinn."

The commissioner took it, dumped out its contents, and sorted through them on his table. "Yes, they belong to a white woman. We found the Irishwoman's body the morning after her death and gave her burial. Her effects and goods will be sold, as her property now belongs to the Queen and the state of Victoria. She had no kinfolk here in Ballarat."

170

Jonathan told the commissioner, "Only Trooper O'Connell. He was sort of related to her."

The commissioner sighed. "We can presume that this blackfellow told the men of the woman's death and that they all went after you at once. It's a great pity that he didn't come to us about the murder."

Jonathan said quietly, "I reckon he thought you wouldn't have believed him if he had. You wouldn't like hearing that one of your soldiers killed her."

The Queen's commissioner's gaze was icy, but he said nothing. He leaned back in his chair and made a steeple of his fingers. Finally, he told Jonathan, "The adult natives won't come back here. They know if they do I shall arrest and hang them. They've done their duty according to their beliefs. I greatly doubt that we shall ever find Trooper O'-Connell's body; but if, as you say, he extorted money from the Widow Quinn, his death isn't any real loss to the Queen's service. You say Mrs. Quinn had the money saved to buy a license?"

"Yes, sir, she'd saved it up."

"Where is it? This money is the Queen's property now."

Jonathan said, "I guess she hid it. I don't know where. I hope you don't think Prince Billy helped kill the trooper. He was with me in the bush all the time."

The man waved an impatient hand. "No, no, I believe you. I've been in Australia for many years, and I know the ways of the natives by now. We won't even try to trail the adult blackfellows though I could summon native trackers from Melbourne. When they hear that these men wore *kurdaitcha* shoes, executioner's shoes, they would probably refuse to track them at all. Those shoes are oval so no tracker can tell if the man wearing them was coming or going." The commissioner smiled thinly and went on, "We weren't aware of your disappearance at first. After we found the woman's body a miner came forward and told us that you and the small blackfellow had vanished."

The commissioner laughed a sharp, strange little laugh. "I suppose you think that the blackfellows did away with Trooper O'Connell to avenge the death of the Widow Quinn, don't you?"

Surprised, Jonathan asked, "Isn't that why?"

"More than likely it is not." The commissioner shook his head. "It's my opinion that the man was executed to put the woman's spirit to rest, so it would not become a wandering ghost. That to the natives would be more important a thing than administering any white man's sort of justice." He motioned toward Prince Billy. "That boy there, I suspect, would tell you the same thing if you could ask him. Well, the two of you will have to shift for yourselves now. I have heard of your father's accident and his death. And now Mrs. Quinn is also dead. What will you do?"

Jonathan said, "I guess I'll look for work with somebody else here till I get enough money to go to Melbourne and work."

The commissioner's blue-gray eyes were hard on Jonathan as he said, "Perhaps I can do you a service, because you did bring O'Connell's horse back to us and surrendered it of your own will. It is a valuable animal, well trained for our sort of work. When Mrs. Quinn's body was found and it seemed you had disappeared, as I said, someone came to me to ask about you. He offered a small reward to find you."

"Who was it?" asked Jonathan in surprise.

"Michael Delehanty."

Jonathan exploded. "I bet he thought I'd hurt Mrs. Quinn and had run away!"

"No, no, you are entirely incorrect. Delehanty expressly said you could not have harmed her. He said that you favored her and she you. He believed you saw her murder and were abducted by whomever killed her. He wanted to see you at once if and when you were returned to Ballarat."

"Wants to see me? Why?"

The man shrugged. "I have no idea. He told me then that the two blackfellows who had been working with him had left his claim and had gone away naked into the night, leaving their garments behind. Knowing something of these people's ways, this led him to believe he wouldn't see them again. He says he wants to see you about something to do with his work here."

"With his work?"

"Yes, it was not for the simple pleasure of your company. Delehanty struck me as a man with something on his mind. Now I bid you and the blackfellow here good night."

Jonathan flared, "I don't trust Delehanty. I don't want to have anything to do with him."

The commissioner said in a weary voice, "You can take that up with him yourself. I sent a trooper to fetch him when you came here with the horse. You'll no doubt find him outside waiting for you. When I send for a man, he comes at once."

"I don't want to see him. He's a convict."

The commissioner said dryly, "Delehanty is now a ticket-of-leave citizen. He has served his sentence, and his past is of no matter to me now. The Queen's justice is done with him."

Jonathan spoke angrily, "And the blackfellows' justice has been done with O'Connell. He was no good. It was his job to hunt for illegal grog tents; and instead of reporting Mrs. Quinn, he blackmailed her. What do you think of that?"

"To answer your question—very little. I have only your word that O'Connell extorted money from the woman. I am now well aware that she operated a sly grog shop, but I do not know that O'Connell took money from her. I know only that he did not report what her actual business was to me. Perhaps he sheltered her because he was her kin. Had he come back here alive, I would of, course, have dealt with him as he deserved."

The commissioner then cleared his throat and said, "Well, I think I've finished with the two of you now. I have reports to write about Trooper O'Connell's disappearance and the condition of his saddle blanket. Go out and speak with Michael Delehanty. It does not matter to me what you two say to one another. But before you go, I want just one final word with you. I don't want to see either you or this small blackfellow before me here again."

Jonathan did not move to obey. Instead he gestured toward Prince Billy and said, "You say you've been here in Australia a long time. Can you speak some of Billy's language? I'd like you to tell him that he can come with me now that Mrs. Quinn's gone. He saved me in the bush. He's my friend."

For an instant a smile crossed the commissioner's grim face, then he said, "Yes, I suspect I can make myself understood to the boy. I did want to ask him some questions about Mrs. Quinn's and Trooper O'Connell's deaths anyway." He turned to Billy and spoke, then asked him something sharply. Prince Billy looked at Jonathan and said something in return. The boy was silent for a moment, then spoke again in a torrent of words.

The Queen's commissioner listened intently, nodded, and told Jonathan, "He understands me. He says you are his friend. He will go with you. He verified that O'Connell was executed by the two men. This boy said he greatly feared O'Connell, because he knew that Mrs. Quinn was going to be killed by him."

Jonathan sighed. "I wish he could have told me that a long time back." Turning about, Jonathan left the tent with Prince Billy at his heels.

# 11

## "Down Under"

As the commissioner had predicted, Jonathan found Delehanty outside the license tent. The man began with, "Boyo,
I want to . . . " but never finished the sentence.

Jonathan cut him off with, "No, mister, I don't want any
part of you. You leave me and Billy here alone!" Hunching
his head between his shoulders and shoving his hands into
his pockets, Jonathan went past the Irishman. He felt proud
of himself for standing up to the old lag.

Now he had to think about how he could earn a living.
The two of them would sleep under a cart tonight, and
tomorrow they'd go up and down the river and creeks,
asking if anybody needed their help. He looked at Billy
limping alongside him and sighed. He was dead sure nobody
would hire the smaller boy, because Billy would not be able

to understand what he was being told to do. But Jonathan knew he owed him a lot. He'd think of him as a partner as long as Billy wanted to stay with him. If the aborigine took a notion to go into the bush and find the men of his band, Jonathan was sure he could do it. He knew he could turn his back on Billy one moment and then find him gone away the next.

In the morning Jonathan thought of going to the Scottish doctor to ask for work but refused to. The man still had not been paid for tending to his father's illness. Instead, Jonathan and Prince Billy began wandering through Ballarat. Day after day they went to the diggings, even to the Cole claim, where two young Australians now worked. The men refused Jonathan's services though he told them he had dug this spot before and knew the claim well. As he turned to leave, Jonathan glanced over the creek and saw that the ramparts of red dirt at the old lags' claim were much higher than they were when he had seen them last. They formed a wall now.

Jonathan had one strange meeting while he scouted Ballarat for work. On the banks of the Yarrowee he encountered the old cook and one of the sailors from the *Wendover*. The cook was as surly as ever. He looked Jonathan up and down, spat, and said, "You haven't grown a inch, kid. You're still runty. Where's your papa?"

"He's dead." To change the subject, Jonathan asked, "Weren't you at Mount Alexander?"

"Yep, we were, but we didn't do too good so we came here to Ballarat to try our luck. We don't seem to be doin' so good here either, so maybe we'll pick up soon and go to Bendigo, the new goldfield."

"Where's the captain?"

"He struck it rich in Mount Alexander and went to Melbourne. We hear he's living like a king. He didn't give any of the gold he found to us, believe me." The cook spat once more and continued, "There's many a time I wish I was back on the whaler, not diggin'. I never thought I'd say that I liked bein' a sea cook, but it beats blisters any day."

Jonathan nodded, "Yes, I think it would." And with Prince Billy trailing him, he went to the adjoining claim to ask for work and was refused again.

For four days the boys went from claim to claim. On the fifth day they canvassed the business houses of the camp, but no one wanted them there either. What money Jonathan had had went for food; and when that was gone, the two of them went hungry. On the seventh day Jonathan decided to see Dr. MacBain. He was busy with injured diggers, so Jonathan waited his turn outside the tent. When he finally entered, the arnica-scented doctor shook his head and said, "I've heard the sad news of the Widow Quinn's murder and of your adventures in the bush, laddie. I've seen ye and the small blackfellow about the camp. What fetches ye to me now?"

"Sir, have you got any work for me?"

"No, laddie." MacBain shook his head. "But I know a man who does. Michael Delehanty. When he stopped me yesterday at the butcher's tent, he told me to tell ye that he wants to see ye."

Jonathan asked wearily, "Him again? Why would he want me when everybody else says I'm too small to hire?"

As he shifted some jars of ointment about on a table,

MacBain said, "Delehanty told me that he seeks ye because of yer small stature."

"Because I'm *small*? He wants me because I'm little?"

"So he said. If I were ye, that would take my curiosity. I'd go find out what a man would want a lad yer size for."

Jonathan said, "The commissioner told me that he put out a reward for me. He must want me bad then."

"Aye, I have heard of that reward. As I said before, I think ye'd best go see Delehanty."

"I sure don't want to but I guess maybe I'd better." Then Jonathan colored scarlet. "I wish I could pay you what I owe."

"Tut, laddie. Perhaps ye can pay me that as well as what I am about to lend ye now." MacBain fished in his waistcoat pocket, took out a sixpence, and handed it to Jonathan with the words, "Go fill yer belly and then go see Delehanty and hear what he has in mind. And bear this in yer own mind too. I still think it would be best for ye if ye were out of Ballarat before summer when the sandy blight comes."

Jonathan bought hot food for himself and Prince Billy at a cook shop, and they ate it leaning against a cartwheel. As Jonathan chewed the tough mutton, he thought about what the doctor and the commissioner had told him. Neither of them seemed to have a poor opinion of old Delehanty, and Mrs. Quinn had even admired him. Maybe there was more to the old lag than the Coles had given him credit for. Besides there was that song about him. He'd often wondered what the words were.

Jonathan muttered aloud, "If he's after me this bad, maybe he'll pay me good wages. Yes, sir, I'll go see old Mr. Delehanty." But as he got up he shuddered, remembering Liam's horrible noseless face. Well if he had to, he supposed he could stand looking at that again too.

It was a beautiful cool day, one of the nicest Jonathan had yet known in Australia. As he and Prince Billy walked through Ballarat to the river, he was thinking of his pa. Not so long ago it would have been he who walked at his side, not a red-shirted Australian blackfellow with a spear. How many changes there had been in the last two or three months! How many things had happened to him. When he woke up in the morning, he sometimes found it difficult to believe that he wasn't in his bed under a warm quilt in the Massachusetts farmhouse. That was where he would like to be. Living in the gold camps of California had seemed quite unreal to him at times, and by now California seemed something he had only dreamed. The voyage aboard the clipper ship came to him in dreams, the few pleasant ones he had.

Once they were on the opposite side of the creek, Jonathan stuck his hands deep into his empty pockets and swaggered, trying to look braver than he felt. Each step he took brought him closer to the Delehanty claim and made his heart beat faster. Red earth was heaped high around it on all sides, marking it off clearly from the claims on either side.

Jonathan stopped at the outer wall of dirt, took a deep breath that filled his lungs to the bottom, and shouted, "Delehanty, it's me, Jonathan Cole! Watch your dog!" How could he forget the dog and what had happened at his first meeting with the old lags?

The deep-voiced call came to him from over the wall,

"I've got hold of Boru. Come inside. The opening's at the corner."

Jonathan found a narrow corridor in the dirt walls and came through it with Prince Billy after him.

There before him stood Delehanty with his hand on the collar of the snarling dog. The man said, "I've been waitin' for ye, boyo. Touch the dog. Let him get the scent of ye, and ye need have no fear of him."

Jonathan asked, "What about Billy here?"

"Boru knows him and the other blackfellows of his band by scent. The boy's been here before."

Jonathan now recalled that he had seen Delehanty nod to Billy occasionally. He stepped forward, touched Boru on the shoulder, and gingerly let him smell his hand and sniff his clothing. Then Delehanty let go of the animal, which went at once to Prince Billy. Jonathan stifled a sigh of exasperation. It would have been far easier for him to come here had he known that Billy had been here before.

Jonathan asked nervously, "Where's your partner?" He dreaded seeing him.

"Liam? In the tent waitin' for ye too. Now let me show ye our claim."

The boy looked warily about him. The small square was crowded with two tents, a larger and a smaller one. Tools were stacked neatly against a tree stump in the center of the camp. What interested Jonathan, though, was the windlass supported by three wooden beams nailed together. A large bucket hung from the rope attached to the machine. Above the windlass was a contraption of canvas that billowed in the breezes like a ship's sail.

Jonathan walked over to the sail, wondering what it was for. At that moment he became aware that someone was shuffling toward him. He turned to see the veiled man behind him. Jonathan held his breath.

Now for the first time he heard Liam speak. The man had a strange hissing voice, but not an unpleasant one. "Na, look below the windlass, dear boyo. Look down under."

Jonathan, less wary now because of the man's gentle tone, did as the old lag bid. It was a mine, the deepest hole he had ever seen. It wasn't like the one his pa and Mr. Mackay had dug, a pit with square-angled sides, or like others he'd seen that were circular. Though this one was circular it was narrow, only about thirty inches wide; and it was spiraled —curving, curving, going deeper and deeper downward.

Delehanty's voice came to Jonathan now. "That's how the blackfellows can dig when they have a mind to. Don't ask me how they dug it. I could not do it even if I could fit meself into the hole. The blackfellows managed it, though. Then they betook themselves away again. I think their leavin' us had something to do with ye, boyo."

Jonathan answered, "It has more to do with Mrs. Quinn than me, but I don't want to talk about it. What do you want with me, mister?"

Delehanty pointed to the deep mine. "We want ye to work for us. We'll pay ye good wages. A brave man could and would dig down there, but he must be small. Liam and I would get stuck, and the hole would fall in. That's where the gold's to be found now in Ballarat, deep down in the earth. The blackfellows know where 'tis found. Liam, show the boyo here what we've got."

As Liam went back to the tent, Jonathan asked Delehanty, "Can you talk with the blackfellows?"

Delehanty nodded, smiling. "Aye, to some I can. I lived with the Kulin for a year before I came here. They're the natives from these parts. I make meself understood among them. Ye may wonder at my not asking the boy Billy to work for us. He could go down into the pit as easy as ye could, but he'd not stick at the digging once he'd got weary of it. The blackfellows have no use for gold. They won't dig for wages but only for tucker and tobacco and finery when they need them. But they know the 'yellow dodger' when they see it. A blackfellow I met up with some months past told me of a cliffside he once saw that had little nuggets of gold in the black soil at the top and in the gray and red clay below. But he said 'tis in the earth far below, in the white and brown clay, that the great nuggets are to be found. He saw them lying deep. All the big nuggets, I think, have been found here on the surface by now. A diggin' man yerself, I think ye know that. Ah, here's Liam back with something to show ye."

As Jonathan watched the ex-convict approach, holding a mining pan in his big hands, he did not fail to catch Delehanty's frequent use of the word "man."

Liam now held out the pan to the two boys. Jonathan could not help but gasp at what he saw, but not Billy, who wandered off and began petting Boru. Thirty or more gleaming nuggets were heaped together. Some were the size of peas, others were as large as hen's eggs. No, these two old lags wouldn't have any trouble paying their license fees for a whole year ahead. Jonathan clenched his fists and his heart beat faster. He felt sick at this great good fortune, which was denied to the Coles.

Delehanty told him, "This is what the blackfellows brought up from the white clay layer sixty feet below before they left us."

Jonathan asked, "How would I get down into your mine? I didn't see any ladder there."

"Easy, boyo! Ye stand in the bucket, and Liam or I lower ye away to the bottom. Ye dig below, and when ye've filled the bucket ye call up to us. We haul up the dirt, look over it, take the gold and dump the rest, and send the bucket down to ye again."

Jonathan pointed to the canvas over the mine and asked, "What does that do?"

"It catches a breeze and sends it down to the man in the mine. There's little air at the bottom. Nor is there much light; ye'll have to work with a candle fixed to yer head so ye can see."

Jonathan shook his head and said slowly, "This one's sure awful deep. My pa was hurt when our mine fell in on him, and ours wasn't anything near this deep."

"No man's is here," said Delehanty with pride. "The blackfellows say the way they dug it this mine will hold, deep as it is. They were wider in body than ye; yet they dug in it and its walls held for them, even when it rained."

Jonathan bit his lower lip. No longer so wary of the old lags, he was wary of the mine. If he agreed to dig, his price would be high. He said all in a rush, "All right, if I do go down for you, I'll be wanting five shillings a day, a place to stay for Prince Billy and me, and food for us both."

185

"Liam, what do ye say to five shillin's?" asked Delehanty.

"Give it to the boyo, Michael! 'Tis fair. The lads can sleep in the small tent with Boru."

Delehanty said, "Then, it's agreed, boyo. Here's me hand on it!"

For a long moment Jonathan Cole hesitated. Then he did a thing he never would have believed he'd do. He shook the hand of Michael Delehanty and then that of Liam. He looked into Liam's veiled face and, feeling he dared say this now, began, "Mr. Liam, I saw your face that one time I came over here. Since I'm going to be working for you, I want to explain why I came. I wasn't really spying on you. I was only afraid that my dog wandered over here and would get hurt." He sucked in his breath and added, "You don't have to wear that veil around me unless you want to."

He heard the veiled man chuckle. "I wear it by day to keep the flies from me face. Until ye've lost a nose like Liam Farley has, ye have no idea how it saves a man from the dust and the flies. I do much regret the day it was bit off."

In spite of himself, Jonathan shuddered. Molly Quinn had been right about how Liam had lost his nose. Some other convict had bitten it off.

Delehanty put in swiftly now, "Are ye ready to go down and have a look about ye? 'Tis a man's work ye'll be doing. Are ye sure ye have the courage for it? If ye don't, we won't hold ye to yer bargain. 'Tis my own guess ye have the stomach for it though!"

Jonathan nodded, "I guess so. Where's the candle?"

"I'll fetch it," said Liam.

Moments later Jonathan wore a band of metal around the

cap on his head. In the middle of the band was a small cup with a spike in it. As he waited, Delehanty put a tallow candle onto the spike and lit it with a twig from the campfire. This done, Jonathan walked to the metal bucket and stepped inside.

Delehanty ordered, "Hold fast to the rope, boyo."

Standing in the deep bucket, Jonathan grabbed hold of the rope that supported it. An instant later Liam began to turn the crank of the windlass, lowering him. He went down slowly, deeper and deeper. His last sight was of Prince Billy's smiling face as the boy knelt at the edge of the pit. Billy clearly thought this must be fun, but Jonathan Cole did not—his heart was hammering in his chest. In spite of his fear he looked closely at the spiraled sides of the pit; he could easily reach out and touch either side. The digging was unbelievably neat. How had the men of Prince Billy's band done this? He'd seen them make the feather shoes and found that remarkable, but this mine was even more so.

As he went down, Jonathan noticed how the layers of earth changed colors. First he saw red-brown turf, then black dirt, then gray clay. Below this was red gravel and red clay. By this time the mine was stuffy. He could hear his candle sputtering and watch its glow flicker. Looking up, he saw only a small circle of blue sky. Moments later the bottom of the bucket came gently to rest on solid ground. The earth around him was white clay, and in it Jonathan saw the marks of knives, where the aborigines had pried out nuggets.

A call floated down from above. "Can ye get out of the bucket?"

Jonathan cried, "I think so." He let go of the rope and

187

gingerly stepped out of the bucket, pushing it to one side. Looking about him, he felt panic catch hold. It was as though he had been buried alive. He wanted to shriek to the men above to bring him up at once. Jonathan fought his fear by leaning against the wall and staring up at the tiny circle of light so far above him now. He thought of the two old lags aboveground—of Delehanty and his torn back and Liam with his ugly, noseless face. What they must have borne! Then, the boy thought of his father being crushed in their own mine. Finally, he thought of the lovely clipper ship and kept his mind on her. Sucking in deep breaths of bad air, he pictured the billowing of her magnificent white sails and the swooping gulls that had perched on her masts.

This began to calm him, and eventually Jonathan looked around the pit again. Yes, he was mighty cramped, but it was possible to dig here once the bucket had been hauled up out of his way.

He heard Delehanty's bellow come down to him. "Get back into the bucket now ye've seen how it is below. We'll bring ye up."

With great relief Jonathan pulled the bucket to him and got inside. A few minutes later he was clambering out of it onto the earth above.

Liam asked him, "Well, can ye do it for us?"

"Yes, sir, it's sure a long way down, but I think I can do it."

Delehanty exploded, "That's a stout-hearted man!" He added, "We'll fill yer belly with Liam's stew, and then we'll send ye down again with a spade and a knife."

"Yes, sir. All right." Jonathan's nose had already scented

the beef bubbling in a black iron pot over the fire. It smelled very good to him. Judging from the fragrance, he thought, Liam must be a good cook.

During the next ten days Jonathan Cole spent four hours of each working day digging down in the deep mine. When he had filled the bucket with white clay, he'd call out "Washing stuff" and either Delehanty or Liam would haul it up. After the two lags examined its contents, they would send the empty bucket down again and Jonathan would begin again to fill it.

Although he'd conquered his fear of the pit, it was a hard place in which to work. The digging was difficult in such cramped quarters; his back and hands ached; and the air was always poor. He not only dreaded cave-ins but the descending iron bucket, which could strike him on the head and stun him. Who would be able to rescue him?

At the end of the ten days he unearthed fourteen nuggets but still had not got through the bone-wearing layer of stiff white clay. He had begun to believe that it went to the core of the Earth itself.

Ballarat had a wild thunderstorm that Saturday night, and on Sunday the skies opened to drench the goldfield with cool spring rains. The old lags' camp became a mass of red mud though they kept the pit dry by covering it with the canvas sail.

Until then Jonathan had kept his distance from the two old Irishmen because he was still wary of them, but during that rainy Sunday he got to know them better.

After he and Prince Billy had supper inside the men's tent, Delehanty sat back with his pipe and started to pass a bottle of rum back and forth to Liam. Neither man drank very much, but the rum seemed to make them more talkative. At first they spoke of Ireland and of how they missed their homeland. In their voices was the same deep sadness Jonathan had sensed in Molly Quinn. Hearing them made him grieve for her and for his dead father.

Suddenly Delehanty asked Jonathan, "Are ye homesick, boyo?"

"Yes, sir, I sure am."

"Ye'd go home to America if ye could?"

"Yes, that's why I'm working for you. To get enough money to go to Melbourne and work until I've earned enough to go home to America."

Liam asked, "Would ye not mind goin' home no richer than ye came here to Australia?"

"No, I wouldn't." Jonathan sighed. "It wasn't my idea to come here anyway." Because they seemed truly interested, he told them of his father's and his mining days in California, the abrupt end to their China voyage, and of the ill luck that befell them in Ballarat. He went on to talk about Molly Quinn, Trooper O'Connell, and how he became involved in their deaths.

Liam Farley said, "Ah, ye've had sour fare here! 'Tis a hard land. Many have suffered in Australia—suffered for doin' less than I in Ireland. There I stole a lamb to slaughter because I'd been ordered off me land; me wife and lads and I were hungry livin' in the hedgerows. They caught me and they sent me here." Suddenly he recited:

> *"They whipped us, they loaded us, they drove us through the Strand.*

*They harnessed us like horses to plow Van Diemen's
   Land.*

"Boyo, we wore chains night and day on our right legs that
weighed four pounds each. We wore suits of black-and-
yellow and had white numbers on our breasts and backs. For
the crown of England we built roads, dug potatoes, cut
down trees, built stone churches and bridges. When there
was naught else for us to do, we broke stones. Oxen, horses
we were, not men at all! And the Queen's prison ships still
come to Van Diemen's Land with convicts as cargoes. Poor
souls."

Delehanty now told about himself. "When I was taken
in Ireland by the Queen's troopers, I was brought to a
ship-prison and stayed aboard her eighteen weeks. Then I
was transferred to another ship and sailed on her for a
four-months' voyage. For seven years after that I worked
on a convict gang. Once I ran away, and ye've seen what
was done to me for that. Men who died under the lash
were buried in their chains, but not me. Michael Delehanty lived! At last I was given me ticket-of-leave. Liam
was given his at the same time, and we came together to
Australia and lived with the Kulin blackfellows until we
got the news of gold here at Ballarat." Delehanty laughed.
"And if we should find the great nuggets, we still cannot
go home to Ireland to buy estates and live like English
lords."

Jonathan said slowly, "Yes, Mrs. Quinn told me that no
convict can ever go home."

"Ah, well, buck up, me dear," put in Liam. " 'Tis not the
same with ye. Ye can go home. They'll have ye back." The

191

man pointed to Prince Billy. "But if ye ever do go, don't think to take that one with ye. He'd sicken and soon die. He has no real need of ye. This country is his."

"I know it is. It sure isn't mine, though." Jonathan reached out to feel the rain beating down on his fingers. He noticed that Boru had crawled inside and had fallen asleep with his head in Prince Billy's lap. The young blackfellow seemed to have a way with dogs, and for a moment Jonathan envied Billy Boru's affection. He certainly had had as little luck with dogs here as with anything else.

Liam spoke again. "I wish I could have known that grand lady, the Widow Quinn, but with a face like mine I saw to it that I never met her. Na, I'd not show meself and frighten her. Nor do I have a wish to be stared at as in a raree-show in Dublin Town."

Jonathan said, "Nobody likes to be stared at."

This made Delehanty laugh. He told Jonathan, "I take it ye refer to me? Yes, I've watched ye for a long time, Johnny Cole."

"I know that you did. Why—because I'm little?"

" 'Tis true, once we had our pit finished yer smallness interested me greatly. But before that I was weighin' yer character. I liked the way ye fought the butcher's lad, who was taller and older than ye. I weighed the character of yer father too. From what I heard him say sometimes to Mrs. Quinn, I found the man weak and foolish, and I wondered how ye would fare with him here in Australia. Ye be made of different stuff. I saw little of him in ye. Na, I doubt ye'll ever be a big man in body, but ye've got the proper mustard in ye."

Delehanty's accurate appraisal of his father made Jonathan sad. He felt this throat closing as he mumbled, "Please don't talk about my pa."

"As ye wish, boyo," came from Delehanty as he put his pipe back into his mouth and, puffing on it, lay back onto some blankets.

In spite of what Delehanty had just said about his father, Jonathan felt strangely comfortable at the moment with the two old Irishmen, Prince Billy, and Boru. He sensed himself part of some odd family group. Jonathan stole shy glances at Delehanty and Liam. The man was not wearing his veil, and Jonathan noted his long, pale, freckled face and mournful dark eyes. How wrong he had been about them. How swiftly he had changed his opinions once he finally knew them. It was hard to believe, but it was true, as true as what Delehanty had said about his father.

On Monday the rain continued until midday, when a watery sun came out in a milky-gray sky. After Delehanty and Liam removed the canvas covering the pit, Jonathan was once more lowered down into it. Rainwater had seeped into the hole, but it was only an inch deep at the bottom. The sides of the mine were no softer than before. Yes, he could work here today.

Three hours later he broke through to the brown clay at last. After an additional half hour of hard, perspiring work, Jonathan Cole spotted a light-colored mass at ankle level in the dark wall. For a moment his heart stopped entirely, and then he was down on his knees, prying frantically with his knife. It was soft, not hard like rock. Taking the candle from

193

his hat, he held it close to the wall. It was yellow. *Gold!* A huge piece of gold, seven or eight inches wide, was jutting out of the clay around it. There was no way of telling its depth because the rest of it was buried in the clay.

Working with shaking fingers, Jonathan jabbed his knife around the nugget to give him a handhold to loosen it. He pried around and then grabbed hold of what he had exposed, trying to pull the mass to him. It would not budge. Once more he jabbed at its edges with the knife, exposing more. This time when he pulled on it it moved. As it did, water trickled from around it.

The gold came out slowly at first. Then all at once Jonathan had it in his hands, its weight making him bend over. The nugget was very large, long and oddly shaped, even larger than the nugget he had seen in the window in Melbourne. This must weigh more than twelve pounds!

Trembling with excitement, Jonathan put the nugget into the bucket and called out the usual signal, "Washing stuff." An instant after the words left his mouth, he was yelling, "Hurry! Hurry!" and scrambling into the bucket on top of the gold. Red water was gushing from the hole where the nugget had been buried. The water level rose with enormous speed. It engulfed Jonathan Cole and the bucket, and extinguished the candle in his cap. Holding his breath, he hung like death to the rope praying he would not drown.

# 12

## Betsy Crawford

Two-thirds of the way up the shaft, Jonathan was no longer able to hold his breath. Liam was managing the windlass but had not caught the boy's urgent shouting over the rushing sound of water. It was not until he saw the water come bubbling over the top of the mine that he began to turn the handle at top speed while yelling, "Flood! 'Tis a flood below, Michael!"

Delehanty came running to work the crank with him, and at last Jonathan rose to the surface unconscious but still clinging to the rope.

Delehanty shouted, leaped forward to catch hold of the boy, and jerked him out of the bucket. Liam ran to turn a barrel on its side and roll it to the windlass. An instant later, while Prince Billy danced up and down in distress, Delehanty had draped Jonathan face downward over the barrel and was pressing down on his back while Liam rolled the barrel back and forth. Water poured from Jonathan's nose and mouth. Then he made a strangling, sputtering sound and began to cough. After a time of rolling he gasped out, "I'm all right! I'm all right! Stop it."

Delehanty flipped him over, sat him upright on the barrel, and stood waiting anxiously for him to breathe normally again. He said, "Boyo, ye are lucky to have yer life at all! Ye must have come across an underground stream that feeds into the creek. There are many of them in Ballarat. Are you all right now?"

Jonathan sputtered some more and coughed again. Then glancing up at the two anxious-looking Irishmen, he said, "Yes, I guess I was lucky. Thanks for getting me up as fast as you could." He shivered and went on, "Have you seen what was in the bucket with me?"

Liam told him, "Na, na, we had our minds on ye, boyo!"

Jonathan coughed, then said, "Well, go look. I sure hope it's still inside." He coughed again and spat out some water. "I think the bucket tipped some while I was coming up."

Leaving Jonathan to Prince Billy, who sat down on the barrel beside him, the two old lags went over to the bucket and dumped the water out. There was a long silence now as both looked into it. Then Jonathan heard Delehanty say, "Holy saints!" and Liam, "Holy Mother of God!"

Yes, the gold was still there. Jonathan, his wet hair plastered across his forehead, looked at Prince Billy, grinned, and said, "I found it! I found a great big chunk of gold way down at the bottom. It just about killed me getting it, but I did! Look at the old lags now, will you?" Even though Billy did not understand, he smiled broadly in response to Jonathan's obvious delight.

Delehanty was holding the enormous nugget, hefting it, handing it to Liam, who handed it back to him. Delehanty said, "This won't go to the gold buyer's tent here, Liam, and be melted down for coins or for jewelry. Na, I'll take it with me to Melbourne right away, where it'll fetch a better prize as a raree-show."

Liam told him in a growl, "Michael, our pit's gone! It's give way at the bottom. The boy can't go down there again."

"Ah, Liam, what do we need with this pit of water now? We're rich as English lords, thanks to the boyo over there and to the blackfellows who dug for us. We'll leave Ballarat and go to Bendigo. What do you think of breakin' up camp once this nugget's been sold in Melbourne?"

"Aye, Bendigo it will be if ye say so, Michael. I care not."

"But first I go to Melbourne with this!" Jonathan noticed that Delehanty was looking at him. "And the Yankee boy goes with me. He found the nugget. He deserves to be shown the sights of the fair city before he leaves for Bendigo with us to dig on another claim."

Jonathan got up, though he felt weak from his narrow escape. "But I don't want to go to Bendigo from here," he protested. "I'll go with you to Melbourne and stay there, Mr. Delehanty, if you please."

Delehanty laughed at him. "Ye've been handsomely paid for diggin'. Do you think ye'll be paid five shillin's a day in

Melbourne? Ye will not. And ye'll not find a ship to take ye to America for the fifty some shillin's we owe ye now. Ye're a good, brave worker. We'd pay ye six shillin's a day to dig for us in Bendigo once we've got a deep mine dug by blackfellows again."

Bendigo? Jonathan sighed and sat down. Another gold camp? Although he hated to admit it, he knew Delehanty was right. He would not be paid such good wages in Melbourne. He was being highly paid now only because he was doing risky work. He was certain in his heart that it would be little Jonathan Cole who would be going down into their next pit.

Delehanty said, "The gold escort rides to Melbourne from Ballarat tomorrow at dawn. I'll get permission from the commissioner to ride behind the troopers and the gold cart. I'll hide the nugget in my saddlebag."

Liam said, "Michael, ye'll be needing horses."

"Aye. I'll buy them with the gold we keep in the pan. Now watch the camp for me, Liam, and dry out the lad while I go to the gold buyer's tent with what's in the pan. Then I'll buy two horses and saddles and the other gear I'll need." Suddenly the man bawled at Jonathan, "Can ye ride a horse?"

"Yes," Jonathan asked sourly, "can you?"

The Irishman roared with laughter. "There's not an Irishman alive who can't ride a horse, boyo."

Jonathan sat disgustedly on the barrel next to Prince Billy as Delehanty carried the huge nugget into the bigger tent and set it on some folded blankets. Then he watched the old lag drop the panful of nuggets into a leather pouch.

All at once Delehanty turned to him to ask, "What shall we name the nugget, lad?"

Jonathan asked in surprise, "Are they named?"

"Some of the of the big ones are. Ye found it, ye name it. Will it be 'Yankee Doodle' or somethin' like that?"

Name the nugget? Jonathan looked at it lying on the blankets. It wasn't beautiful. If it had been made of wood, it would have been fit only for firewood. Only its yellow color and the fact that it was undoubtedly gold made it appealing. Looking at it, he thought of his dead pa, whose own golden dreams had failed here, and of Mrs. Quinn, who had also failed and died in Ballarat. The gold should rightly be called the "Curse of Ballarat"; but no one would ever understand that name because few men besides himself, he was sure, considered gold a curse. His hairsbreadth escape from death made him look at the nugget with revulsion. It could so easily have killed him.

His thoughts went again to Molly Quinn. Maybe he should call it the "Queen of Ballarat" in her honor. No, for him there was already too much talk of queens here in Australia. But somehow it should be named for her. He thought back to the day he had first met her and of what Trooper O'Connell mockingly had called her then. He said, "I'll name it the 'Angel of Ballarat'. That's what I heard a man call Mrs. Quinn one time."

Delehanty and Liam looked at one another, and both nodded. Delehanty said, "Good! The 'Angel of Ballarat' it will be. Now, boyo, dry yerself and wash yer clothing. Ye want to look yer best to meet the girls of Melbourne when we see the sights of the town."

With another laugh Delehanty left with the leather pouch of nuggets. Jonathan looked after him sadly, wishing it had been Charlie Cole rather than Michael Delehanty who had struck it so rich here. Finding the great nugget would have been the most important moment in his father's whole life. How his face would have shone with joy! Instead, Charlie Cole's son had found it for the two old lags. He was tied to them now and would soon travel with them to a new gold-field. Would he ever be able to leave Australia?

Jonathan began to remove his wet garments. When he later heard the clopping of hooves signaling Delehanty's return, he came out of the tent wrapped in a blanket and peered between the piles of dirt. Jonathan watched the Irishman ride up on a black horse, leading a saddled sorrel. He dismounted and tethered the horses to a gum tree outside the ramparts. After removing their saddles and bridles, he brought the gear into the camp and dumped it beside the larger tent.

Jonathan asked him, "Will Billy go to Bendigo with us?"

"Who knows? Liam and I will keep him with us so long as he chooses, but I doubt he'll stay for long. Someday he'll go off to join the men of his band. He might even wander off while we are down in Melbourne. I think he stays here now because of ye, Johnny, not because of us. He was not often here when the men were digging but went off to be with the Widow Quinn and ye."

"I guess that's so," said Jonathan.

That evening, to Jonathan's surprise, Michael Delehanty took a Melbourne newspaper out of his pocket and handed it to him. The ex-convict said, "Neither Liam nor meself can read. We never learned, because the English government would not permit Irish children to be taught to read when we were young. Can ye read?"

"Sure I can. I had to go to school for a long time."

"Ah, how lucky ye were in that!" exclaimed Liam Farley.

"Aye," Delehanty agreed, "just think on it! Men can take most things from ye but never yer education. Now, read the paper to us—every word of it, mind ye I want to know what to see in the city of Melbourne."

"Everything?" Jonathan was amazed at the request; but at the man's nod, he lit a candle and by its light read the paper through. He read everything aloud; the news of the world, the advertisements, the notices of ships arriving and departing the port, the names of passengers aboard, the theatrical amusements, the lists of horses running in various races, the prices of wool.

"Ah, 'tis grand to be able to do that!" exclaimed Liam when Jonathan had finished the last column of the last page.

"Aye, lad, we owe ye for the entertainment," came from Delehanty, who smiled contentedly.

"Mr. Delehanty," said Jonathan after a long silence, "I bet you have a good singing voice. Weren't you the one who sang the song about the wild colonial boy one time when I was living over the creek?"

"Aye, boyo. That's an Australian song."

"I know that. Do you know any Irish songs?"

"I do. I do." And now Delehanty lifted his gray head and sang several ballads that Jonathan found beautiful—sad and lovely. But the old lag did not sing the one song the boy wanted to hear.

Jonathan dared say now, "Mrs. Quinn told me that there was a song about you. Would you know that one, sir?"

"Aye, lad."

"Will you sing it now?"

Liam asked softly, "Michael, are ye willing?"

"Why not?" said Delehanty with a laugh.

The tune was beautiful and so was the Irish tenor voice that sang it; but Jonathan could not understand the words. Delehanty sang it in Gaelic. The boy thought he knew why —it was so the ballad about an Irish convict would not be understood by the English jailers. He did not ask to have it translated, for he sensed Michael Delehanty would not have liked to. But Liam told Jonathan quietly, "It says that Michael took more lashes from Black Robert, the Queen's flogger, than any other man. Where other men died, Michael lived. 'Tis a song a man who witnessed the floggin' wrote in Michael's honor. There's a part in it too about the blackfellow women who looked on and wept in pity."

"Ah, Liam, that's enough of that. Ye speak as an old woman would," growled Delehanty. " 'Tis time the boyos went to bed. Good night to ye both."

Jonathan and Prince Billy went into the little tent they shared and lay down side by side. For a long time Jonathan lay awake, listening to the mating calls of springtime birds and asking himself what his life would be like in Bendigo. Would he have to fear the return of the sandy blight there too? He suspected he probably would since Bendigo was not too far from Ballarat and so had the same sort of summers.

All at once Jonathan became aware that Prince Billy too was awake. The native boy didn't say anything; but his small hand came out and briefly grasped Jonathan's wrist, as if Billy sensed that he was fearing the sandy blight and had to keep Jonathan's hands from his eyes.

"It's all right, Billy," said Jonathan. "Don't you worry. It'll be all right. We'll go to Bendigo and take our chances there too the same way we do here. Maybe I'll get a hat with a veil to protect my eyes. You know, Billy, sometimes I do think you read people's minds. If you do, you ought to know that I sure do like you as a friend even if we can't talk a lot together."

Liam Farley cooked breakfast for them at dawn. Jonathan ate in silence as he listened to a kookaburra bird braying to the yellow sunrise. Delehanty was in a fine humor. He told Jonathan, "I remembered last night that I have an old mate in Melbourne, old Tom Crawford who was with me in Van Diemen's Land. He's married and I hear he's got a daughter, Betsy, who'd be just yer age, I think. We'll have to look old Tom up when we get there. Now, finish yer tucker and we'll be off to the commissioner's tent, where the gold cart and the troopers'll be waitin'. Say good-bye to Liam and Billy now."

Jonathan did as he was directed and shook both Liam's and Prince Billy's hand. He then went out with Delehanty. Jonathan mounted the sorrel and gathered up the reins while the old lag put the gold nugget into a large leather saddlebag and securely buckled straps over it. Then Delehanty got on the black horse and without a glance at his claim left it at a trot.

Before Jonathan followed him, he looked behind and saw

Prince Billy standing outside the dirt mound, watching him. He had his spear with him and lifted it. As he did, he pointed to his open mouth, where the tooth was gone.

For a moment Jonathan held the sorrel in and, opening his mouth, pointed to his own lost tooth. He supposed this was the way aborigines said good-bye. Then he turned the horse about and urged it into a jolting trot to catch up with Delehanty.

They found the gold cart waiting in front of the commissioner's tent and the troopers mounted up beside it. Jonathan watched as the official came out of his tent, pocket watch in his hand, and spoke to the trooper in charge. Both nodded. Then the next moment the soldier gave the order and the cart's driver whistled to his team. The gold escort started at a trot through Ballarat, and Delehanty and Jonathan followed behind the last soldiers.

Once they were outside Ballarat, the lead trooper shouted another order. The driver of the cart lashed his horses into a gallop as the soldiers began to surround it, their swords drawn and ready.

Jonathan clung hard with his knees to the horse. He had not ridden for so long that now he had to focus his whole attention on staying atop his horse. On and on they galloped, passing travelers bound for Ballarat. People fled to the sides of the road just as he and his pa had once done. At first Jonathan tried to count the hills on the road to Melbourne but at last gave up the effort. He was too busy trying to keep his horse from stumbling into a rut to pay any attention to the scenery. Riding so hard had at first been exciting, but Jonathan soon found it only straining.

When they halted at midday in a flat open country that offered no shelter for bushrangers, he felt light-headed with weariness. As he was dismounting, he noticed that the troopers sheathed their swords and took their carbines from their saddle scabbards. They then made a circle of armed men about the gold cart. Their faces were hard beneath their visored caps.

As he walked his sorrel beside Delehanty's black horse, Jonathan looked again and again at the troopers, thinking of O'Connell. How many times had that man been a part of the gold cart's guard? Many times, he was sure; and yet he'd been a criminal demanding money from Mrs. Quinn.

Delehanty asked Jonathan now, "I see ye eye the troopers, boyo. Do ye know any of them?"

"No, sir, but I was thinking of Trooper O'Connell."

"Aye, that one. I'm sorry the blackguard was an Irishman. I knew he was the trooper who checked business tents for proper licensin'. But I thought he kept Molly's trade a secret from the commissioner out of friendship for her just as the men who drank at her grog tent did. It does not surprise me that the commissioner did not know what Molly sold. He relied on reports from O'Connell. As the Queen's representative, he himself is far too important a man to go to a trade tent and rub elbows with common diggers."

Delehanty said with a growl, "I think, if the truth be known, ye'd find that the soldiers ye see about the cart here may have shared in the money O'Connell took. He probably made the rounds of Ballarat's sly grog tents for that very purpose. The Widow Quinn's was not the only one. Mark my words, the hard ways of the commissioner and some of

205

the trooper lads will soon bring bloody sorrow to Ballarat. The diggers are wearying of their high-handed manners."

Jonathan said sourly, "I don't take to queens. At home a president is a lot like other folks. Pa once shook the hand of President Martin Van Buren."

"Aye," said Delehanty with a snort that made his horse shy, "a man does not shake the hand of a king or a queen."

"Mr. Delehanty, what would you have done if Mrs. Quinn had told you she was paying O'Connell?"

"Boyo, if she had not been too proud to ask for help, I would have given her the money to buy her license. Then I would have gone to the commissioner and told him what O'Connell was doing. I would not have harmed the trooper myself though I would have liked to. You see, I obey the laws here. I've already had me fill of Van Diemen's Land."

Delehanty laughed aloud. "Just think upon it! Here I am travelin' in the company of Queen's troopers with a great fortune in gold with me. When I was transported to Australia for pullin' an English soldier off a horse because I saw him strike a woman, I did not have a farthin' of me own. How strange life can be! A man never knows what's to happen next."

"I guess that's true enough." And Jonathan sighed.

Hearing this, Delehanty told him, "Buck up. Ye'll soon be seeing the sights of Melbourne and that will make ye feel better. I'm glad to be goin' there, and so should ye be, Johnny Cole. . . ."

Delehanty would have gone on about Melbourne, but at that moment the order to mount up was given, and they were off again at the same breathless gallop.

There were two more rest periods during the day. By now Jonathan was weary and walked his horse in silence beside Delehanty's. His thoughts were somber; how little pleasure he took in the prospect of visiting Melbourne. He would just as soon have stayed in Ballarat.

They came clattering into Melbourne near sunset, and here Delehanty and Jonathan parted company with the gold cart and the soldiers. As the two of them rode their tired horses at a walk through the city, Jonathan was amazed at how Melbourne had grown since he had seen it last. Some streets now boasted stone buildings, not just brick ones. The thoroughfares were thronged with prosperous-looking citizens going home from their day's work.

Jonathan had expected to go immediately to an inn, perhaps the famous Lamb Inn that had been advertised in the newspaper. Instead they rode through the center of the town down to the Yarra Yarra River and crossed on a ferry-raft over the stream in silence. By now it was dark, and Jonathan was wondering why Delehanty had not taken his great nugget to a bank or to some other safe place in the city. But he didn't question the man.

Once they were over the Yarra Yarra, Delehanty and Jonathan both remounted and on they rode, heading south, away from Melbourne. By now Jonathan guessed that the man planned to spend the night at the house of his old friend from Van Diemen's Land.

Still they rode on, passing the last of the dwellings. Jonathan recalled that beyond them were only warehouses and wharves. Why go there? Did Tom Crawford live on one of the abandoned ships as people did in San Francisco harbor?

They finally came to Queen's Wharf, where the *Wendover* had berthed so many months ago. Jonathan felt sadness engulf him as he looked at the long line of deserted vessels in the harbor. Only two were still occupied, carrying lighted lanterns at their bows. It was to one of these that Delehanty rode and dismounted. He gave the reins of his black horse to Jonathan to hold and went up the gangplank swiftly. A man came out on deck to greet him. Crawford, of course. The two men spoke softly, so the boy could not hear what was said; but he saw the stranger nod.

Then back came Delehanty to say, "Boyo, this is where I leave ye!"

Suddenly Jonathan thought he knew what Delehanty was about to do. A second glance showed him that this wasn't a ship where a family lived, but one that was going to sail away. Its masts had sails furled tight to them, ready to be shaken free for a voyage at any time. Jonathan knew Delehanty's game now. He cried, "You're taking the nugget aboard this ship and running out on Liam. You're cheating him! Why did you make me come with you?"

How Delehanty laughed. He said calmly, "Na, na, how could ye think I'd do me old mate any harm? Get down now and let me show ye something."

Still suspicious, Jonathan sullenly got down from his horse. Leading his sorrel and Delehanty's black, he followed the man to the bow of the ship.

"Look now, boyo," ordered Delehanty. "Read the words there."

Jonathan looked at the bow and read aloud, "Betsy Crawford." The name belonged to this three-masted schooner, not to a girl at all.

Before he could say anything, Delehanty took a leather bag from inside his jacket and handed it to Jonathan. Then he took the reins of both horses from the boy and said, "As I said, this is where I leave ye! There's golden guineas in there. It's wages Liam and I owe ye, and more—far more. I've already paid for yer passage to Canton, China, aboard this English ship. The man on deck told me that she is indeed the *Betsy Crawford* though I cannot read her name meself. He says that from Canton ye can get a Yankee clipper ship bound for America. Now go aboard; this ship sails in the morning."

Jonathan exploded, "But how did you know about her?"

Delehanty laughed. "Ye read all about her to me last night in the newspaper. That is why I fetched the paper to ye, I wanted to see if there was a ship ready to sail to America or China. Now get ye aboard.

"Don't get the idea that I paid yer passage because I look upon ye as a grandson or any kin of mine. Na, I did it because ye've also suffered and ye have whined to no man of it. Liam wants ye to go home too. We think yer havin' seen two deaths that mattered to ye is enough for a boyo yer age. Ye've come near to losin' yer eyesight too. No young shoots should come to diggin's anywhere. Gold, not scarlet, is the devil's own color, and this is the devil's own land. It's me lot and Liam's to stay here, but it's *not* yers. We old lags were transported here, and so in a way were ye. I'm giving ye yer ticket-of-leave right now.

"We never meant to have ye dig for us in Bendigo. That was said only to see if ye would whine, and ye did not. Go home; no one can keep ye here. Ye are not like Liam and me. We are prisoners still because we cannot go home.

"Ye can read. Go to a school in America that'll fit ye for a better life than that of a digger. Learn what a man can do that is not measured by his size. I heard ye say to Liam once that ye might like to be a sailor. Na, not good enough! Be a master of a ship, if it's ships ye fancy. Be master of yerself! Use yer brains in yer life, not yer muscles and yer back. It is a sharp head and courage, not size, that will take ye very far indeed. Don't be a miner like yer father. Ye'll never find a nugget so large again as the 'Angel of Ballarat'; nor probably will I. But I'm not young, so it matters not to me. I'll look for more gold to keep meself amused."

Jonathan did not answer. He was looking at the schooner and thinking, weighing it against the life he was certain he would have if he went to Bendigo. A voyage to China? He would really be going there after all.

He made up his mind. Yes, he'd go home—but by way of China. Home to Massachusetts and his aunts, and back to school. He knew he would be able to handle any bullying after all he had been through since he left home. He'd do what this man he'd once hated advised him to do. If this brave man thought him a man, so would other men, less esteemed than Delehanty. "Master of himself" Delehanty had said just now.

All at once Jonathan thought of whom he was leaving behind—his friend, Prince Billy. He asked, "Does Billy know that you had it in mind to send me home?"

"He does. I told him ye might leave us and sail away. He said to me that he would not want to live as a stranger in yer land."

Jonathan nodded. So that was why Billy had grasped his

wrist last night and this morning signaled with his spear and pointed to his mouth. It was to say a real farewell. The boy said, "I'm glad he knows. I won't ever forget him. I won't forget anything or anybody I knew here down under."

"Na, it may all dim a bit for ye in later years, but ye'll not forget. I'm told ye Yankees are sometimes called Brother Jonathans, but to me ye'll always be Johnny Down Under, because of what ye did for us in our mine. But who can tell; perhaps ye'll come back here again someday."

Jonathan boasted happily, "If I do come back, it'll be as master of my own ship!" He stuffed the leather bag of money into his pocket, grabbed Michael Delehanty's hand, and squeezed it as hard as he could. He then turned and strode up the gangplank of the *Betsy Crawford*. The boy ran along the deck to the ship's rail and looked down onto the dark pier to wave farewell.

But old Michael Delehanty wasn't waiting. He'd already mounted his horse and, leading the other, was riding off the wharf with the "Angel of Ballarat" at his right knee.

Jonathan nodded. He did not call after Delehanty but watched him out of sight, fixing him in his memory.

There went a man whom gold would never own. Well, gold would never master him either, not Jonathan Down Under. Fatherless and alone in Australia, he had survived. From now on, whatever he decided to do with his life and wherever he might go, he'd be his own man—forever!

# Author's Note

*The Gold Camps of Australia*

Most Americans know of the 1849 gold rush to California; but relatively few, I have found, have heard of the great gold rush in Australia, beginning in 1851 in the state of Victoria. There were a number of Australians mining in California in 1849 and 1850. One of them, having learned prospecting in America, went home to Australia, looked for gold, and found it. The Australian gold rush was on once the news was released. Ballarat, Mount Alexander, and Bendigo were the first prominent Australian goldfields; gold was discovered at Castlemaine later.

Though Americans, Charlie and Jonathan Cole would not have been so very unusual as participants in the Aus-

213

tralian gold rush. People of every nationality flocked there, hoping to become rich. By 1856 there were at least 10,000 Americans in the Australian diggings or in business in Melbourne. Many of the Yankees stayed, and their descendants now tell visiting Americans that they had a Yankee great-grandfather.

The government of the state of Victoria kept good order in the diggings. They were policed by troopers who were sometimes renowned for their officious brutality. Trooper O'Connell would have been quite in character for the times. Licenses were renewed each month to keep digging. The fee set was 30 shillings, which is roughly $50.00 in 1980 U.S. currency. This was no small sum. Gold was sold to the gold buyer for £3 16s per ounce, or roughly $120.00 U.S.

Many diggers could not pay the high fee. If they became derelict in their payment, they could be imprisoned. Such conditions and the growing resentment of the diggers led in 1854 to the famous affair of the Eureka Stockade in Ballarat, a battle that pitted soldiers against miners.

What I have written about routine camp life in Ballarat and about the various mining methods is factual. By American standards Australian mining claims were very small, only twelve feet square. In some camps eight feet was the norm, and miners had to pitch their tents a distance from where they dug. Sunday work was forbidden. There was a sunset gun signal.

Down-under miners first panned in the rivers and creeks. Then they built rockers; and finally they dug mines. This was the usual pattern in the United States as well.

However, Australian nuggets are not like American nuggets. By our standards some of the nuggets found in Australia are simply enormous. They are usually found well below the surface.

Some mines in Ballarat were shallow, others very deep; and they were usually very narrow. One pit only twenty-four inches wide by sixty feet deep yielded an entire ton of gold. Experienced miners from Cornwall dug some of the deeper holes, some one hundred and seventy feet down. Others were dug by aborigines who indeed could dig in a spiral fashion that the Caucasian miners could not manage. According to old-time Australian diggers, the spiraling guarded against cave-ins. Mark Twain, a visitor to Australia, commented on such spiraled mines and wondered at them.

To give an idea of the richness of the Australian goldfields, from 1851 to 1853 Ballarat alone produced $300 million worth of gold. This was more gold than all of the California fields had brought forth together.

Mining was dangerous then, as it is today; and it was just as perilous in Australia as in California. Cave-ins were common. So were floods; and in deep Australian holes, sudden breakthroughs of subterranean springs sometimes drowned miners.

Social life in Ballarat was as crude as in California and consisted in both places of grog shops (saloons) and cheap dance halls. In Victoria an establishment that sold liquor had to have a license. Many grog sellers did not have the money to buy one, so they operated "sly" grog shops that could be raided and burned at any time by order of the camp commissioner. Some grog sellers hid their illegal trade by conniving with the police (troopers). The beverages served in Ballarat would have chiefly been rum or gin, but mixed drinks such as Fench and Spider were served, as was the remarkable Knocker of Ballarat.

I have referred to an actual eye disease. In 1851 it was called sandy blight. I believe it is trachoma. The treatment for trachoma was horrendous; in 1851 it was treated exactly as it had been in ancient Egypt. The treatment consisted of daily scrapings under the eyelids with a bluestone, a crystal of copper. The disease was a summer one transmitted by dirt and swarms of flies. Some miners wore veiled hats to protect their eyes from the myriads of insects.

Camp food was boring to say the least, chiefly damper (soda bread), beef or mutton or anything edible that could be hunted, coffee, and dried fruit.

## Australian Society in 1851

It may seem that I have made much of former convicts in this novel, but a good proportion of the population of 1851 Australia was indeed made up of former convicts and the descendants of earlier ones. After the American Revolution the English began to send men and women convicted of "lesser" crimes such as forgery, arson, and petty theft to Australia instead of to America. (Murderers, assassins, and highwaymen were hanged in the British Isles, not transported.) A person could be transported for stealing a very small item and even solely for the crime of speaking out against the English government. Many Irish were transported for political reasons. Others came during Ireland's Potato Famine of the 1840's, because, starving, they stole in order to be caught, imprisoned, and fed by the British.

Molly Quinn and Michael Delehanty would not have been such unusual citizens of Ballarat. (I have written in the book of a fictional character who stole thirteen boots. This was a real crime, for which the English ancestor of one Australian librarian I know was transported in the early nineteenth century. She had no idea why he would steal thirteen *boots* and swore that it was not thirteen *pair!*)

The state of Victoria was never a penal colony as was New South Wales, but released convicts from New South Wales and from Van Diemen's Land (modern-day Tasmania) went there. The last shipload of convicts came to Van Diemen's Land in 1853.

Prisoners were reputedly very harshly treated there. Floggings were common, and many men died under the lash. Leg chains were worn by male convicts, and forever after such men could be picked out by their strange, swinging stride. Convicts thought to be informers, betrayers of their convict mates, were often attacked and had their noses bitten off.

A convict given a pardon or ticket-of-leave, the preliminary step to a full pardon, had to promise he or she would never return to the British Isles. If a former old lag went home he or she was sent back at once to Australia. Several attempted to return, but most were apprehended and brought back.

## The Aborigines

The first European adventurers to explore Australia found not only reversed seasons but strange trees and never-before-seen animals (such as the kangaroo, wallaby, koala, platypus, and goanna) and birds (the emu, currawong,

galah, lorikeet, and kookaburra). They found species of
opossums and owls and what appeared to be a handsome
canine but was really a completely wild dingo. To this day
a dingo puppy cannot be truly domesticated.

These same explorers also found natives, the aborigines,
sometimes called blackfellows. Nomadic, they wandered in
bands and did not know the languages of other bands. The
Kulin inhabited Victoria in 1851. The aborigine words in
the story are Kulin. Though the natives used spears, boomer-
angs, knives, and started fires with drills, they did not have
the bow and arrow. They were often kind to white settlers,
fond of children and generous-natured white men. A rite of
manhood involved knocking out the right front upper tooth.

Like other primitive people living at a Stone-Age level of
civilization, the Australian natives were known for unusual
mental powers. They could sometimes predict events. They
had very sharp hearing, could mimic animal cries extremely
well, and were superb hunters. They were even said to be
able to "smell" a snake nearby.

Aborigines were intensely religious, believing that many
inanimate objects, such as hills, mountains, and rocks, had
spirits of their own. They were very concerned with ghosts;
and therefore my fictional natives could have tracked Molly
Quinn's murderer in order to lay her spirit to rest. The
oval-shaped shoes made of emu feathers were called *kurdaitcha*, or executioner's shoes. Along with actual chains
worn by convicts of old and a flogger's lash, I saw a pair of
*kurdaitcha* shoes in a museum in Katoomba, New South
Wales.

Like the American Indians, the aborigines were not
treated well by the incoming white settlers, though they

Author's Note

were not enslaved. Sometimes the natives killed the imported sheep and were hunted down and shot or fed poisoned flour. Aborigines considered the kangaroo their own and could not understand why, if the white man killed their kangaroos, they were not entitled to kill his sheep.

Today's aborigines live in cities and on what Americans would call reservations. Some are cowboys. Others have adapted to Australian society of the 1980's; but their alcoholism and suicide rates unfortunately correspond to that of American Indians, also very high.

In writing *Jonathan Down Under* I have asked my personal physician, Dr. Gershen Schaefer, and my ophthalmologist, Dr. Richard Rosenberg, for information about the treatments for pneumonia and for trachoma in 1851. I wish to thank them for their research in my behalf.

A number of libraries supplied materials for this novel, among them the University of California, Riverside library; the Riverside Public Library (with a special thanks to Shari Haber); the library of Macquarie University, North Ryde, Australia; the University of Melbourne library, Melbourne, Australia; the National University Library at Canberra, Australia; the Mitchell Library, Sydney, Australia; and the library of Sovereign Hill Goldmining Township, located near present-day Ballarat. Sovereign Hill is a re-creation of an old Australian gold camp and well worth the visit.

Patricia Beatty
December 1981

219

Now a resident of Southern California, Patricia Beatty was born in Portland, Oregon. She graduated from Reed College there, and then taught high-school English and history for four years. Later she held various positions as science and technical librarian and also as a children's librarian. Quite recently she has taught Writing Fiction for Children in the Extension Department of the University of California, Los Angeles. She has had a number of historical novels published by Morrow.

With her late husband, Dr. John Beatty, Mrs. Beatty also coauthored several books. One of them, *The Royal Dirk,* was chosen as an Award Book by Southern California Council on Children's and Young People's Literature. Subsequently, Mrs. Beatty received another award from the Council for her Distinguished Body of Work.

Mrs. Beatty is now married to a professor of economics at the University of California, Riverside, and has a married daughter, Alexandra Beatty Stewart.